COPP
FOR
HIRE

Also by Don Pendleton

THE EXECUTION SERIES
THE ASHTON FORD SERIES

COPP FOR HIRE

A Novel By

DON PENDLETON

DIF

DONALD I. FINE, Inc.
New York

 Published in the United States of America by Donald I. Fine, Inc. and in Canada by General Publishing Company Limited.

Library of Congress Catalogue Card Number: 87-81420

ISBN: 1-55611-064-2

Manufactured in the United States of America

10 9 8 7 6 5 4 3 2 1

This book is printed on acid free paper. The paper in this book meets the guidelines for permanence and durability of the Committee on Production Guidelines for Book Longevity of the Council on Library Resources.

First Edition

For Cy, for Frank, for Don,
and for all the good
gentlemen of law and literature
who helped this book into print;
my gratitude.

CHAPTER ONE

I SMELLED TROUBLE all over this kid the instant she stepped into my office. She was hot. About twenty. Designer jeans so tight they could sweat. Shrink-wrapped onto a highrise bottom and grafted onto the vee, low on the hips to reveal an indented little belly button, flaring a bit around three-inch heels. A tube-top started about six inches higher up to cover another four or five inches of delectables. On some girls maybe it would have covered ten inches vertically; on her, four or five. I'm talking tits... mouth-watering tits, thrusting against the elastic material in a way designed and intended to grab the attention. But they had a lot of competition. This kid was great everywhere. Long black hair spilled onto creamy shoulders. The face was... exotic, I guess. Lips that gave you a stir every time they parted, eyes that looked everywhere and seemed to see it all. I figured they'd seen quite a bit already.

I also figured hooker or stripper, or maybe both.

My snap judgments have been known to be wrong, but I did not think I was wrong on this one. She looked the office over, looked me over, almost went back out, finally asked in a husky little voice, "Are you Joe Copp?"

I looked the office over, looked her over, pushed my nameplate to the edge of the desk. "That's me."

Guess she decided to give me a try after all. She dropped onto the edge of a chair, looked around again like a bird casing the territory before relaxing onto the perch. "I think I'm in trouble."

Knew damned well she was in trouble. Any kid walking around looking that edible was in trouble.

I asked, "Who is he?"

She asked, "How did you know?"

"Instinct?"

She said, "I don't know his name. But I think he's a cop."

I told her, "So'm I. Maybe you need to see a lawyer."

The kid was very uptight. She frowned, looked at the door as though wishing she'd never come through it, said to me while looking at the door, "No, I—you see . . . you are a private detective, aren't you?"

The lettering on the door says that. Well, what it says is *Copp For Hire,* which is also what my business cards say and what the godawful expensive yellow pages ad says. A small conceit. I was a public cop for eighteen years. Still think of myself that way except that now I have private sponsors.

I told this kid, "Yes I am. But I don't guard bodies or settle disputes between lovers."

She stared at me for a few seconds then replied, "This is not like that. But maybe I should see a lawyer. Could you recommend one?"

"What is it like?"

"What?"

"You said not like something. So what is it like?"

She fumbled in her purse for a cigarette. Gave me a stir as she inserted it between those ripe lips. I got to my feet and went over to light it for her. She rose quickly to accept the light, gazed into my eyes briefly then turned away to release the smoke. I am six-three. In the heels, this kid's eyes were level with mine. She smelled nice. But she was looking at the door again.

I told her, in a voice as gentle as I can make it, "You can leave any time you'd like. Relax. I'm not going to jump your bones. Sit down and tell me about it."

She dropped abruptly onto her perch again, waved the cigarette in a dainty grasp. "I don't want to leave. I think he might be out there waiting for me."

I went to the window and looked out, saw nothing unusual. "Looks clear to me. What's the beef?"

"There's no beef. Not that I know about, anyway. This guy just follows me around all the time. Everywhere I go."

I sighed and asked her, "Are we talking official police business here or . . . ?"

"Well I hope it's official business. I haven't done anything wrong. But why would he be following me?"

"Why do you think he's a cop?"

"George said—he's a bartender where I work—George said he has seen this guy in a police uniform. But he's never in uniform when I see him, and—"

"Where do you work?"

"New Frontier."

Uh huh. One of the joints in the county jurisdiction. You've seen them. *Live Girls, Girls, Girls—Totally Nude*.

"You dance there?"

"Yes."

"You've seen this guy there?"

"Yes. Started coming in a couple of weeks ago. Always sits in the back, though, never up along the runway. Never tips me. Just sits there and stares at me all the time I'm performing. Then he leaves. Guess he's worked out the timing 'cause he comes back in every time I go on. For the past week I've been noticing him sitting in his car when I get off work. He follows me home and I think he sits outside and watches my window. I think he's a freak, and I'm scared. Yesterday he followed me to the mall. I saw him twice while I was shopping."

I returned to my chair, sat back, put my hands together, asked the young lady, "Is there some reason why you should be under police surveillance?"

She gave me a blank look and a negative wag of the head.

"Do you do drugs?"

"I might toke once in a while. But nothing..."

"Live alone?"

"I have a roommate...a girl. We share an apartment."

"Do you know anyone who's dealing?"

"Half the guys you meet nowadays deal *some*. But I've never—no, I don't really know anyone that involved."

"You have no other, uh, activities that would be of police interest?"

"If you mean do I make dates out of the club—no, I don't."

I smiled. "Had to ask."

She replied simply, "Everyone does."

"Do the other girls make dates? At the club, I mean."

"Some, I guess."

"Your roommate?"

"She doesn't work there."

"Where does she work?"

"She does parties."

"What kind of parties."

"You know—birthdays, bachelor parties, that kind of thing."

"As a stripper?"

"Yes."

"Does she do other things?"

"I wouldn't know about that."

"Or care?"

"Or care," she confirmed, with another suck at the cigarette.

I told her, "I'm expensive."

"How expensive?"

"Just like a hooker," I replied. "Hundred dollars an hour plus expenses."

She said, "Jesus," and bit her lip. Then I got the first smile out of her. Not much, but a wry little twist of the lips. "*Cheap* hooker," she said.

I smiled back. "Well, I don't give as much. What do you want me to do for you?"

She got to her feet. "Nothing. Can't afford you."

I told her, "The public cops work for free. Go tell them your troubles."

She said, "Guess I'll have to. But I'm as scared of them as I am of the freaks."

"No reason to be, if you're straight. I was a public cop. Never jumped any little girls' bones."

That earned me a second smile, this one a bit more honest. "It's not my bones I'm worried about."

That comment could have meant several things. I wanted to know what it really meant, so I said, "Tell you what. I'll give it an hour for you. If I scare the guy off, maybe you'd like to give it an hour for me."

She did not reply to that, except with the face. So I'd been fifty percent on target. You win some and lose some. I felt like I'd won all of this one, though, by losing.

I told her, "Just kidding. But you can buy me a drink, maybe, and reserve me a spot on the runway. What time do you go on tonight?"

"Be there at ten o'clock," she said, but not with a lot of enthusiasm.

I said, "Hey, I had to get the straight of it. Okay? So now I'm straight. Won't cost me anything to drop in and have a talk with your freak. Except the price of a drink. Spring for that and we have a deal."

I got a whole smile that time, a quite dazzling one. "Deal," she said, "but it's a two-drink minimum. It'll cost me six bucks."

"You can take it off your taxes."

"What taxes?"

She gave me a smile, a handshake, and a polite goodbye.

Then she took that tantalizing body out of there. I was crossing to the window to check out her car when I heard the squealing of tires digging hard at asphalt and the groaning of an internal-combustion engine at heavy takeoff demand.

The unmistakable *whump* came instantly. I got to the window just in time to see that ex-tantalizing young body flying through the air all a mangled mess; a dark vehicle speeding out of the parking lot.

I knew even before I went out there that I had just lost a client. A client, yeah. A deal is a deal, and I owed her at least that hour I'd promised.

But as I knelt there beside that broken corpse, the feeling came and very strongly that I would be spending more than a mere hour for this one. As it turned out, I very nearly spent the rest of my life.

CHAPTER TWO

I MIGHT AS WELL tell you right up front. I'm a hardcase, and everyone I've ever dealt with knows it. Not that I mean to be that way. I'd a lot rather coast in the slow lane. Take life as it finds me, you know. I must have a ten-foot stack of travel magazines in my living room. Buy them compulsively. Never read them. Just buy them. And there they sit. But it seems like I never do. Every street has two sides, you know. I'm always on the hard side, and it seems like I'm always moving along it.

Don't get the wrong slant here. Not looking for sympathy. Don't deserve any. Just want you to know who I am. I'm Joe Copp, a cop for hire. I have always been a cop for hire, all my adult life, and I'm closer to forty than I like to think about. Started in San Jose eighteen years ago. Graduated to San Francisco three years later, lasted five years with that force, went on to City of L.A. for another five and finished off at L.A. County. I've done it all. Traffic, patrol, vice, narc, robbery, homicide—even took SWAT training at L.A.

I never really "moved" voluntarily. But always for the same reason. I have a habit of becoming unpopular. Finally decided to go into business for myself. But I'm still unpopular. Respected, I think—or I like to think —but nobody really likes me. That's okay. I don't give a shit if they like me or not. Respect is enough.

I changed wives, too, every time I changed jobs. Same reason. I'm a hardcase. Or so they all think. Actually, if they only knew, I'm a pussycat. Sucker for a sob story. The problem, you see, is that I *look* like a hardcase. Not my fault. I was born looking like this. Don't know how to look any other way, not even when I'm feeling kindly and gentle. Guess I don't speak softly, either, but I really do try sometimes. Last wife told me I'm great in bed, every woman's savage dream, she said, but how much time could we spend there. Well... I could have spent a lot more time there than she did, so I don't know about that savage-dream stuff. As for bringing flowers and remembering anniversaries... who the hell has time for that on the hard side of the street? Sometimes I don't remember my own name.

Okay. So maybe they're all right. I'm a cowboy, a hardcase. Can't turn it off and tuck it away until the next watch. Can't turn it off for the department politicians, either, or for the media people or police critics and sobsisters. And I guess I never really strained my eyes to read a guy his rights after a hard collar. So I'm the kind of cop that's always in trouble. That's okay, too, because while I'm being so candid here I might as well tell you—I'm more comfortable on the hard side of the street, so I guess that's why I always seem to be over there.

I say all this up front so you maybe will understand how I am feeling when the traffic boys come to check out this hit and run. These are traffic *boys*. They should be guarding school-crossings. From the looks of one of them, he should still be *using* a school-crossing. They are very soberly fussing with steel tapes and measuring distances, going through their routine like a classroom drill. They've roped off the area and covered my ex-client with a yellow tarp. I know the routine. They are really killing time and trying to look busy doing it, waiting for a detective to show up, waiting for the coroner's office—securing the scene until someone with some authority arrives to take over the investigation.

So I don't tell them a damned thing. Except I heard the screech, saw the victim flying, saw a car taking off at high speed. They are not asking the right questions, anyway.

My office is in a small business complex. I share the area with a hairdresser, a cosmetics shop, a real estate office, a dentist and a chiropractor. It's all ground level. Each business is accessed directly from the outside. The parking lot and driveways take up more ground than the building does. There's a self-service gas station on the corner, right next door, and a 7-Eleven store behind it. You can gain access to our lot from both the gas station and the 7-Eleven.

Way I reconstructed the hit, the guy was idling in the little access lane from the 7-Eleven, just waiting for my girl to show. He had to be on full alert and ready to jump the moment she emerged from my office. There are no sidewalks. You step out of the building directly onto the parking lot. He would not have had a shot at her if she'd been parked right up front. So he had her car spotted and knew that she'd have to walk across to the next parking aisle. He was alert. He was ready. He nailed her. And he must have accelerated from a standing start to something like fifty mph in about five seconds. Which means a high-performance engine. I was guessing a TransAm from the flash glimpse I'd had of it.

The traffic boys did not ask for my reconstruction. They did ask if I could identify the victim, which I could not since she had not given her name, but they did not ask if I knew anything about her or why she had been at that particular spot at the crucial moment. I volunteered nothing. Which is not against the law. I did do a sneaky thing, though. The victim's purse had gone flying with the body, spilling its contents over a trail about thirty feet long. I spotted a key ring peeking out from beneath a car parked near my office door. I gave it a gentle nudge with my foot while the traffic boys were comparing their sketches, then kicked it into a flower bed.

The detective never showed. The coroner's man did and almost immediately released the body for transport to the morgue. The traffic boys scooped up the purse and its scattered contents—all that was obvious—then took down their ropes and went away.

I couldn't believe it.

I mean, that was an outrageously sloppy operation.

So I did their job. I canvassed the complex for eyewitnesses and I asked questions. I found a woman who'd been waiting to see the chiropractor at the time of the incident. She eyeballed the car as "very powerful and shiny black with some kind of design along the side." A guy in the real estate office gave about the same eyeball but a bit more specific about that "design." He said the car had "flames" painted on the hood and side. An oriental lady who manages the 7-Eleven told me that the car had been "parked" in the access lane for about five minutes. She said the driver was a man wearing dark sunglasses.

Then I went back to that flower bed and picked up the key ring. It had four keys on it, two of which carried a *Ford* logo. Six Fords were parked out there. I scored on the fourth try, an old Thunderbird; found the registration and other ID in the glove box. Her name was Juanita Valdez. She would have turned twenty in a week, and she had lived about five minutes away from where I stood.

I jotted down the address and returned the registration to its neat little repository, then locked the car and went to my own.

Apparently she'd lived very modestly, as most kids her age are required to unless they have help from affluent parents. The car was old and the apartment building was older. It was not a security building, sat right on the street in a low-rent area, had no off-street parking for the tenants.

I had a creepy feeling as I cruised past the entrance but I didn't know if that was caused by the building or by a glimpse I had of a dark car rounding the corner at the next intersection. I opted for the latter and got down there as quickly as I could in four o'clock traffic. Saw nothing there to induce quivers so went on around the block and found a parking place, went into Juanita's building. Main entrance was not even locked, though it was equipped for it. I tried the keys just for the hell of it and, yeah, one of them fit.

It was a three-story walkup. The number I was looking for was at the top, rear. This door was locked and I had the key—but, damn, I also had a return of that creepy feeling as I let myself inside.

Good enough reason for that.

The place was a wreck. Furniture turned upside down, cushions slashed, litter everywhere. I waded through that to the kitchen for more of the same, then into a small bedroom for even worse.

But the real booby prize was waiting for me in the bathroom.

She was probably roughly the same age as Juanita, almost as pretty, just as dead.

She wore open-crotch pantyhose and nothing else. She'd been hogtied, gagged, worked over and strangled with a G-string, probably her own.

And I wondered what the hell I'd stumbled into here, on the hard side.

CHAPTER THREE

IN MY BUSINESS, you either develop a neutral stomach or it retires you early. Mine went neutral a long time ago and it had worked on nothing since breakfast, so I was hungry as hell when I headed back to the office. I'd spent most of an hour going through the mess in that demolished apartment; found and pocketed a few small interesting items but left everything else exactly as I'd encountered it and quietly got away from there.

But I was hungry. May sound callous, considering the moment, but a neutral stomach does not recognize such moments and mine was clamoring for me to send something down. Anything. I have no gourmet tastes. I stand six-three, as I said, and weigh two-sixty but I do not eat ritually or fancily. I just send something down when the belly demands. I also do not have much body fat. The frame is big and the bones are heavy. I try to do an hour a day on the track to stay in tune and maybe that much a week with my judo master to keep the black belt and the humility intact. Humility, yeah. My master is seventy-five and weighs about a hundred pounds. I have yet to beat his ass, or even to come close.

Anyway, the stomach was yelling at me so I pulled into a coffee shop two blocks from the office and had a quick dinner. I didn't get back 'til about six. Two detectives were waiting for me in an official car parked right beside my door. I knew one of them. Too well.

L.A. County provides police services on a contract basis to some of the smaller municipalities, like mine, that cluster about the big city. Police jurisdictions can be a nightmare in this area, with so many towns and cities jostling one another in crazy-quilt patterns and with no clear demarcation between them. I mean, you can drive along one avenue for five minutes and pass through wedges of half a dozen different municipalities. So things could be a lot worse than they are if each of those towns insisted on maintaining their own police departments. My city council did it the smart way. Turned it all over to the sheriff and let him juggle payrolls and health plans and pension plans and political infighting. We pay an annual fee for the service.

By and large, the service is good. But like all big government departments, "by and large" covers a lot of not so good.

Gil Tanner was not so good. Sloppy soft, beer belly, a guy who'd long ago lost pride in his profession and in himself; liar, cheat, manipulator, sleazebag. All in all not a character to inspire confidence in the law. Scared hell out of me, in fact, any time I thought about a jerk like this walking around with a badge and a gun.

So that was who was waiting for me. Along with a younger version probably already well along that same road; mean-looking little prick, the kind who'd drag a collar into an alley and beat the shit out of him with a baton just for kicks.

Don't tell me it's pure accident that cops like these gravitate to beats like this one. Somebody up there knows what they are and does not want ever to have to look on them. Why the hell can't these departments police themselves instead of just shoveling the shit aside until something shockingly rotten *makes* them look?

Which was what was running in my mind when I spotted those two. But it started off amiably enough. Tanner opened his door and swiveled about with his feet on the pavement as I walked up.

He said, "Joe, you old shitbag, long time no see. How's it going with private enterprise?"

I lit a cigarette before I met his gaze and replied to that. "I don't know where it's going," I told him. "Sure as hell isn't coming my way. You assigned to the hit-and-run?"

He balled his fist and made what was intended as a

humorous honking noise into it; a raspberry with gesture. "Belongs with the fucking traffic detail. Run our asses up and down this pike all day long on this asshole stuff." He jerked a thumb. "Meet my partner, Ed Jones. Just came over from the reserves. I'm breaking him in."

I waved to the little prick and he waved back without much enthusiasm.

I said to Tanner, "Must be special material if they gave him to you." That has a double meaning, you know. Probably was not lost on Tanner. He's a sleaze, sure, but a smart one. I was sure, too, that he'd already filled Jones in on the kind of horse's ass I am because the guy had not yet learned to be as two-faced as Tanner; he'd been giving me a solemn inspection the whole time, probably wondering how many raps of the baton it would take to send me to my knees. I was looking straight at the kid as I added, "Looks to me like a guy who'll have no trouble at all soaking up every rotten trick in your sleazy bag."

Tanner decided to take that as a compliment. For the moment, anyway. He laughed nastily and told me, "Well, we make 'em or break 'em around here. But you know all about that, don't you, ex-Sergeant Copp." He put heavy stress on that *ex,* as though I would not get his meaning without it.

I said quietly, "Yeah, it's a great force, Tanner. What can I do for it this evening?"

"What was your business with the Valdez girl?"

"That her name?"

"Cut the shit. Tell me about 'er."

I showed him both palms as I replied, "You have her name. That's more than I had. I eyeballed it, yeah, or part of it. Heard the tires screeching—not braking, accelerating—heard the hit. Looked out the window in time to see her fly by. Black sedan. Gave the report to your traffic boys."

"You called it in, too."

"Sure. Wouldn't you? The kid was lying there all broken and bleeding No... that's an unfair question, isn't it. Maybe you wouldn't. How'd you work the call, Tanner? Write up your report from the traffic investigation?"

I must have been right on target. He moved too quick to cover it. "You know we can't work them all at once, and I haven't filed my report yet. You reading this as a deliberate hit?"

"You want to quote an ex-sergeant?"

"Maybe."

I sucked on my cigarette, dropped it, stepped on it. "It sounded that way, yeah."

Jones had stepped out of the vehicle and come around to join the parley. He said to me, "We'll bust your ass quicker than you can cover it if you play games with us, Copp. This old-soldier bullshit doesn't buy you a thing."

I looked from him to Tanner, and I guess that "hideous smile" I've heard others talk about joined me in the look. It sent Tanner leaning away from me; he spoke from the deep interior of the car. "Shut up, Ed," he growled; to me: "He's frisky, Joe—forget it."

I said to the frisky recruit, "Little unusual to come straight from reserve to detective squad, isn't it?"

But the prick suddenly was not looking directly at me. Probably thought I was addressing his partner, and was content with the thought. Tanner answered for him, anyway. "You know how it goes, Joe. Feast to famine. Right now it's famine. So Ed got lucky. He's doing good, really good."

I said, "With that mouth, he'd better do better than that."

It became a laugher.

We stood and jawed for a few minutes. Never again returned to the investigation. As soon as it was graceful to withdraw, they did.

But you can see, can't you, why I did not volunteer any information to those guys. I mean, there's a limit to how far you want to go with guys like those. I actually had never meant to conceal anything from the official investigation. Why would I want to do that? It just worked out that way because of the circumstances.

I'm sure I would have gone straight downtown and laid the whole thing on the appropriate desk before the night was over. Nobody would have faulted me if I'd done that. We're talking about a few hours here.

I could have been downtown by eight o'clock easy.

Would have been there, too.

But I walked into my office and found déjà vu.

Some son of a bitch—or some sons of bitches—had gone in there and torn the whole place apart, emptied all my files onto the floor, turned out every drawer, slashed all my beautiful leather-upholstered furniture—I mean pure leather, the real stuff—even bashed into the hollow core of the door to the washroom.

They say I have a truly hideous smile when I am upset.

I must have been smiling like Long John Silver himself when I went out of there and set sail for the New Frontier.

CHAPTER FOUR

IT'S A LOW-SLUNG BUILDING occupying the corner of a busy intersection up in the foothills. Like I said earlier, a county area. That does not mean it is in the country. The patchwork of communities I was talking about do not always come together at neat boundaries. Sometimes there is a narrow buffer zone between the incorporated areas. So these unincorporated wedges or slices are governed directly by the county board of supervisors. In L.A. these are your traditional free-trade zones—which means that most anything goes, so long as it doesn't get too flagrant.

The New Frontier was pretty damned flagrant.

Big place. Legal capacity of probably several hundred patrons. Open from ten in the morning 'til two in the morning seven days a week. Gold mine.

Kind of joint where the parking lot always seems to have as many pickup trucks as passenger vehicles. And you don't see Pierre Cardin or Gucci fashions in there. You do see a lot of dirty jeans and cowboy boots. But the owners are smart. They police themselves. Bouncers are probably their heaviest payroll.

All of the girls double as cocktail waitresses and dancers, take turns on stage—and of course the stage runs everywhere; it's actually the bar, sort of star shaped; most of the seating is there. So the girls work you from both sides; as bare-assed dancers directly above your head and as technically bare-assed waitresses at floor level. I would have to say that it is all prime. The amateur night, held once a week, is actually a showcase for hopefuls trying out for jobs—auditions, if you will—and from what I hear the line never ends so I guess the management can be choosy.

It was only about seven o'clock when I blew in there, but the parking lot was already half-filled. The place was a dark hole. It would be fair to say that all the lighting there was came from above the stages, and that was mostly blue. Twenty or so girls were wandering about in various degrees of undress and pushing the drinks. One total nude was gathering up discarded bits of fluff and money from the stage and making her exit while an unseen emcee was announcing the next dancer, "the bewitching Belinda." Canned music with a throbbing disco beat catapulted the bewitcher on stage dressed in cowboy boots and hat and nothing else.

I stood just inside the door for a moment letting my eyes adjust to the lighting; turned away two girls who wanted to seat me, which brought a bouncer over damn quick.

"You'll have to be seated if you wanta stay. Two-drink minimum."

"Mind if I wait 'til I can see the seats?"

"The girls know where they are. Come on in and party. You can't stand here in the door."

"Actually I came to see George."

"Thought you wanted to see the seats."

"That, too, yeah."

Belinda had just thrown a leg over a patron's shoulder and was playfully riding it like a bronc, waving her hat overhead and yelling *wa-hoo*.

"George who?"

"She's something else, isn't she."

"No freebie looks, pal. Either come on in or turn around."

"George the bartender. He's working tonight, isn't he?"

"Sit down and order. I'll send him over. But the girls are better."

I said ha-ha and let a harem girl lead me away. She sat me down squarely in front of Belinda, who by now was kicking off her boots and moving into overdrive. It looked as though I had been chosen for her next prop; she bumped in and wiggled her crotch at my face but I leaned back and caught her eye. She caught the uh-uh in mine and moved on down the line to pull another guy's face into her belly.

The girl who had seated me leaned into my arm and massaged my back with a practiced hand as she invited me to relax and have fun and what was I drinking. One of the unspoken but unbreakable rules in these joints: the girls can touch you anywhere with anything but you keep your own hands off of everything. I have found the whole scene to be an exercise in frustration but I guess a lot of guys don't mind the teasing.

I ordered a Jack Daniels and George; received two Jack Daniels and no George about thirty seconds later. Another unspoken and strongly observed rule: move the drinks and move them fast. Turns out here that booze from the well and even a beer costs you three bucks per, but four-fifty gets you a name brand, Jack Daniels or whatever. I gave the harem girl a ten and she returned a single, but slowly; I told her what the hell to keep it and asked again about George.

She said George didn't know me but I told her I knew Juanita and I had a message from her for George.

So a minute later I get George.

George is about twenty-five. George is a flaming gay. I get a whole new insight now into the little joke at the door with the bouncer. But he seems a nice enough guy.

"Terry said you have a message from Juanita. Is she sick?"

"About as sick as you can get, yeah. She won't be coming in tonight."

"These girls, these girls. So unreliable. They're driving me crazy."

"You the keeper of the harem, or something?"

He has a good laugh. "I'm the duty eunuch, yes. I do their scheduling. So what's wrong with Juanita this time?"

"Broken bones. Compound fractures, both arms, both legs. Also lost her face and probably several vital organs."

"You are not being very funny."

"Don't intend to be. Juanita is dead."

"Good lord!"

"She was killed outside my office today. Came to me for help. Didn't give her any. Should have. I am upset about that. Very upset."

"Who are you?"

I handed him a card. "Who's the guy?"

He examined the card, softly asked. "What guy?"

"The one that's been bugging her. You told her a cop."

"I told her nothing of the kind."

"Sure you did. Who's the guy?"

"I told her I *thought* I had seen the man before. In

some kind of uniform. A security guard. A policeman. Something like that. Why in the world did she go to you about this?"

"Because she was scared out of her skull, that's why. With good reason, as it turns out. Who's the guy, George?"

"I told you I don't *know.*"

"Think again. Harder."

"I'm going to have to ask you to leave. This is a place of business and I have work to do."

I produced a pad and pencil, handed it to him. "Address and phone number, please. Catch you tomorrow."

All this, you know, was under very difficult circumstances. The music was very loud. Patrons were hooting and yelling now and again when Belinda did something especially imaginative. The lighting was terrible to start and getting worse all the time, going now to strobes sequenced to the beat.

George refused the pad and pencil. He pivoted about and walked away.

I went after him, about three paces to the rear and lurching just a bit with maybe a touch of vertigo from the strobes. Ever been in one of those? There's a very unreal quality, everything you can see all weird and slo-mo, the damned "music" flaying away at you.

With all that, though, George must have been able to get off a high-sign to the bouncers because I suddenly had two of them sandwiching me and herding me toward the door.

Please understand. I didn't go in there for trouble. I can get a bit single-minded, though, at times. I guess this was one of those times. I was pissed, understand. Pissed at myself because a cute kid died after sort of hiring me to look after her. Pissed at sleazy cops. Pissed at perverts who enjoy carving on cute kids and beautiful furniture. Pissed at the whole situation, I guess.

But I was not pissed at those guys for doing their job.

So I set them down gently and went on to put the collar on George. I had to haul him over from the back side of a high-production bar, though, and I guess it spilled some bottles and broke some glasses.

Which brought more bouncers. Four more.

So we broke up a lot more stuff.

Then I dragged George outside and gave him another crack at the memory cells in clear air.

That seemed to help.

"Honestly, I don't know his name," he gasped from two feet above my head. "I just remember something about . . . he was a reserve deputy, or something."

Yeah. The clear air helped a lot.

Didn't do much for my mad, though. Well . . . maybe it did focus it just a bit.

I went away from there looking for a hot dog who

loved to play cop enough to do it for free and enjoyed cruising around in a TransAm with flame decals—a little prick, probably, who enjoyed the official privilege of throwing his weight around and terrorizing people who couldn't fight back.

I knew where to look, yeah.

CHAPTER FIVE

IT WAS A TYPICAL WEDNESDAY EVENING at the substation. The deputy on the desk was Charlie Hall. Never had any problems with Charlie. Good cop, did his job and collected his pay, spent most of his free time with Big Brothers and Pony League and Little League and every other kid thing he could spread himself onto. Must have been about due for retirement but I knew he'd never walk out on his own; they'd have to carry him away kicking and screaming. Some cops go a little crazy with the stress. Cops like Charlie just mellow into it and divert the stress into positive outlets.

He looked up with a delighted grin. "Joe! How you doing?"

I assured him I was doing fine but I'm sure he knew

by the ripped jacket and the mouse under the eye that I was doing the same as usual.

We small-talked for a moment, then I asked him, "Who is this new cop on the block, Ed Jones?"

Charlie gave me a smile and a wink. "You mean Buck Jones."

I growled, "Buck always wore a white hat. I believe this guy qualifies for a different color."

Charlie kept right on smiling. "Don't ever turn your back on him, Joe."

"He's riding with Tanner. They should have a lot of fun keeping each other in sight."

He chuckled. "I rode with Tanner once. One whole miserable week. But don't give the guy all black marks, eh? He's a smart cop."

"Too smart," I said. I was craning for a look at Charlie's log. "Who answered the call on the Valdez homicide?"

He tightened just a bit. "You chasing ambulances now, Joe?"

"Not hearses, for sure," I told him, then sat down and lit a cigarette. "If Tanner's working swing, how come he got Valdez? That should have come in on day watch."

"Joe. When are you going to give up those goddamned cigarettes? They cause heart disease, emphysema, cancer—they'll even make you impotent."

I said, "I never heard that."

"Heard what?"

"Impotent."

"Oh yeah. Anything that needs good blood circulation to function properly. Nicotine constricts the blood vessels. Been having trouble lately getting it up?"

"Getting it down," I said. "How come Tanner?"

He glanced at his log, sighed, took a deep breath. "Joe, you're not with the department anymore. I can't talk official with you."

I said, "Bullshit."

He said, "Actually the call came down just right before shift-change."

"And?"

"And we're spread thin right now. Would've had to dispatch a car from one of the other districts, and they're all thin too right now."

I said, "Charlie, I can't believe you just sat on this waiting for the new watch to get on board."

"Didn't say I did that, Joe, did I? Actually Tanner called in and said that he was on it."

"He wasn't dispatched."

"No. Said he was in the neighborhood and in touch with the traffic detail. So I logged him in."

I said, "Great. The sleazebag never showed. Not until some time around six o'clock."

Charlie said, "Couldn't be. Traffic detail released and departed shortly after four."

I said, "That's right. And they made a carbon of their report for Tanner. He never showed, Charlie."

"Couldn't be, Joe."

"Okay, it couldn't be but it is. Where can I find him?"

"You mean right now?"

"I mean right now, yeah."

"Go home. Take a shower. Change clothes, at least. Talk to him tomorrow."

"Now, Charlie."

"Right now, huh."

"You got it."

He sighed, turned to his console and did some things with the buttons, came back to me with, "He's on a private call."

I blew smoke at him. "What do you mean, private call?"

"You know. Moonlight call."

I said, "Wait. Cop for hire doesn't do it when the cop's already on watch. Give me that again, just so I have you clearly."

Charlie frowned, took a couple of breaths. "Some of the guys nowadays, Joe, on a slow nightwatch, take private calls to relieve the boredom."

"Bullshit on the boredom. If they take them, it's to relieve the financial statement. I can't believe things have got that loose."

"Lots of things are loose," he said with a tired smile, "since you were here. I didn't make the game, Joe. I just sit here and watch it."

I gave my hideous smile, I think, and asked, "Where is he?"

"Officially, I don't know."

"Unofficially?"

"His call came from this joint up above foothills. He signed down for thirty minutes."

"When?"

"Just about thirty minutes ago."

"New Frontier, right?"

"You were always a jump ahead, Joe."

At the moment I was feeling a few jumps behind. I thanked my pal Charlie and headed for the door. But he called me back before I could get there. Something was working on the console. He'd put on the headset and was taking something down; took a moment to tell me from the corner of his mouth, "If you're headed that way, change your mind. Tanner just requested backup units. We've got a shooting at New Frontier."

I was not about to change my mind.

I was pounding along the hard side at full-tilt, and I knew it. I think I'd known it since late that afternoon. There was no turning back now.

George, the bartender and duty eunuch, lay sprawled on the tarmac outside the joint with two ugly bullet wounds in his face.

An ambulance and a couple of squad cars were there and the uniformed cops had their hands full with crowd control. I brushed right on past them and went to stand over the victim alongside Tanner. The paramedics already knew that they were wasting their time there but they were observing the routine just the same and preparing for transport. I caught a glimpse of Jones poking around inside the cab of a sporty Toyota pickup as Tanner said to me, "Satisfied now, asshole?"

"Satisfied with what? He was alive and breathing last I saw him."

"Heard you roughed him up pretty good."

"Heard wrong. Didn't even muss his hair. Who did?"

"Figured maybe you could tell me who did," Tanner said with a nasty smile.

"Figure again."

He produced a vinyl evidence bag and held it in front of my eyes. A snub .38 pistol was in there, typical Saturday-night special. "Look familiar?" he asked me.

"Yeah. I've seen a thousand just like it."

"This one," he told me, "has had the serial number removed. It also has been fired recently and there are two empty cartridges in the cylinder."

"Neat," I said. "Convenient. Where'd you get it?"

"Ed found it in that pickup over there."

"Yeah, that's really neat," I said.

"What the hell do you mean by that?"

"You know what the hell I mean by that."

I left him standing there and returned through the police line to my car. One of the bouncers I'd encountered earlier was standing there looking at it as I walked up. He looked at me and I looked at him. He sort of half-smiled; said, "You're a cop. Sorry. I didn't know."

I said, "You still don't know," and got in the car.

He walked away while I lit a cigarette. Before I could kick the engine over, though, the door on the passenger side opened and a very cute person slid in beside me. It was Belinda Buckaroo.

I said hi and she said hi.

Then I said, "Where are we going?"

And she replied, "Wherever you want to go. Just do it quickly, please."

I asked why and she told me why.

"That's my car those cops are tearing apart," she said.

"The Toyota pickup?"

"That's the one."

So yeah, we went on along the hard side together, at full-tilt. I've had better company. But not very often and maybe only a shade better.

"Why me?" I asked her, a mile down the pike.

"You're the guy that tore up the club, aren't you?"

I said, "Well, I had some help."

"I know who you are," she told me. "I know all about you. I recommended you to Juanita."

"Juanita is dead," I told her.

"I know about that too," she said, face tight. "George told me."

"When did he do that?"

"Just about sixty seconds," she said, "before he got out of my car and got his head blown off."

"The Toyota pickup."

"That's the one," she told me again.

The hard side, yeah. There are those times when you simply cannot avoid it. And there are times when you don't want to.

CHAPTER SIX

HER NAME WAS REALLY LINDA SHELTON, age twenty-five, blond all over and beautiful all over the full five feet and ten inches—and she was working her way through college. Actually. I know; you get that from all of them, hookers and all; in this case it was true. You just knew it was true without even having to question it. Bright, sharp, well-spoken and poised; I probably would have believed it if she'd told me she was on sabbatical from a nunnery.

She took Belinda because it was alliterative with bewitching and because you played the theatrical games even at this level of theater.

She had these great eyes, you know. Very expressive. All sparkly and dancing when she was excited; snap, crackle and pop when mad; smoky and mysterious when feeling amorous. But I'm getting ahead of it here.

I took her to my place because it made no sense to take her anywhere else. I have a nice place. Surprises a lot of people. But I always tended to put my money in my home. Home is where you become yourself, you know. Whoever you are, whatever your dreams, your home tells you who you are and what you think of yourself. That's my theory, anyway. I know a lot of people who never found that out. They think they find themselves at work, or at play, or off chasing the dream whatever it is. Not true. You find yourself where you live. Looked at your place lately? Look at it. It'll tell you damn quick who you are, if you really want to know.

Linda knew that, I think. She began looking at me through different eyes the minute we got there. "This is really nice, Joe," she said as I escorted her through the Grecian entryway. It's a colonnade, but sort of on the mini-side, with diffused lighting. Variety of potted plants to take away the starkness of the marble look.

Bought the place five years ago. *Started* buying, of course. If I stay lucky I just might live long enough to finish buying it. Not many people, I think, look at it that way these days. Like buying a car. Never expect to pay it off. Just keep trading it off. My car I paid off two years ago. Still runs good; looks okay. My place will still look okay twenty years from now, too, and I'll *own* the sumbitch.

I've got a split-level entry inside, four steps in Italian

tile that lift you to the reception hall. Off to the left and down again is the kitchen and all the utility space; off to the right and up again is the living and partying space. A single bedroom takes up the whole back area —why would I need more than one?—but it's more than a bedroom, actually. I've got a spa back there and a small workout gym. One corner is my home office. Whole thing overlooks the San Gabriel Valley and half of the communities in the area.

Linda seemed to love it. And I was getting a bit instant-smitten with Linda.

After the proud tour we returned to the kitchen and I put the coffee on. She kicked off her shoes and pulled both feet into the chair with her and sat there glowing at me.

I said, "Well."

She shook her head, kind of wonderingly.

I asked, "Do I intimidate you?"

"Should you?"

I shrugged. "I get it all the time. This may surprise you. But women often find me a little scary."

She laughed softly. "Surprises hell out of me, Joe."

I told her, "I suppose you intimidate a lot of guys."

She gave me a look of mock horror. "Please. You're messing with my livelihood there."

I said, "Tell me about that."

"About my livelihood? Woke up at age twenty and realized I was headed absolutely nowhere. Signed up for night classes at Citrus and struggled along that way until it dawned on me that I would get my degree when I am forty. So I found night work and became a full-time student."

"And now you're a graduate student."

"By golly, I think he's got it."

"What're you going for?"

"A Ph.D. in behavioral psychology."

"Why?"

"Because I find people fascinating, and because a wise man once told me that every life should be lived with fascination."

I said, "Damned few are."

She said, "Maybe that's why we need behavioral psychologists."

I asked her, "Do you use what you've learned in your present work?"

She smiled, looked down at her body. "I use everything I can find."

I told her, "I'm not being nosy for personal reasons. I'm reaching for some understanding here. How's the money at the New Frontier?"

"Money's great," she replied soberly. "I've cut back to a twenty-hour week and I still do okay."

I needed a better handle than that. "How great is okay?"

"Great enough."

"Look, I don't want to be indelicate but I need a picture here."

She looked at her hand and picked at a long tapered

fingernail as she replied, "A smart girl can clean up there, Joe. I don't mean that she has to sell anything more than voyeurism." She raised those great eyes into an electric contact with mine. "I average a couple hundred in tips for a four-hour shift."

I whistled softly. "But you're smart."

The eyes fell. "No. Juanita doubled that, easy."

"By being smart."

"By doing what she figured she had to do. Look... a guy drops in on his way home from work for a couple of expensive beers and a cheap thrill. He might toss a dollar bill onto the runway and he might not. Another guy comes in because there's simply no place else he can get the kind of attention he finds there. He's lonely; he's probably shy and maybe unattractive, and he's desperate for attention. He discovers that he gets special attention if he's laying a five out there to attract the girl. And very special attention for a ten or a twenty. The girl might even put her fanny in his face and take his picture while she's dancing along."

"See many of those kind of guys?"

"Oh yes. I had a sweet old man used to come in every Tuesday night and lay down a hundred-dollar bill for me. I started giving them back to him, when I could. Juanita would not have dreamed of giving it back. She would have worked that little man for every dollar he had. But as I said, she figured she had to. Most of her money went to her family in Mexico. She was supporting about twelve of them."

"You said give it back when you could. When couldn't you?"

"Takes a bit of discretion, Joe. We are not working just for ourselves, you know."

I waited.

"You think the management would be content with three-dollar drinks while the girls are walking out with all that money? The house gets half."

"That's shitty—"

"No, it's business. Everybody is in business to make money. You know that, Joe."

"So this two bills a night you're taking home represents only half your actual take."

"Forty percent. I said the *house* gets half. Another ten percent goes into the kitty for the rest of the help. Bartenders, bouncers, like that."

"A guy gives you a tip because he likes you, not the rotgut he's drinking."

"Yes, but the guy wouldn't have that chance to like me unless someone else was paying the rent and providing the support facilities. They have quite a payroll there, Joe."

"Bouncers alone," I said sourly, "yeah."

"Speaking of which,..." she said, giving me a warm once-over, "you really walk pretty tall, don't you."

I hung my head in exaggerated false modesty. "Forgot myself." But I really appreciated that admiring look. I quickly added—not just to change the subject but because I really wanted to get the picture—"So if you have to split the take, I gather there is something beyond an honor system to police that take."

"We're out there stark naked, after all, when the dance is done. Where could we hide it? Besides, there are eyes everywhere."

"You said *smart girls,* though."

"Yes. Well. Where there's a will there's usually a way, isn't there?"

I guessed it and said it: "And Juanita was knocking down."

She shook her head. "I don't know about that."

"But you told me you sometimes managed to get the little man's bill back to him. How'd you manage?"

She blushed. Actually blushed. "Well . . . ," she said, then laughed softly.

"So it can be concealed, even stark naked."

"A single bill is easy enough," she said, the color still hanging in there. "Especially if you're a little damp at the time. Have to gather up your costume too, you know. You can make the switch."

I grinned. "*I* couldn't, no. So you get a little damp sometimes?"

"Damn it, Joe. Back off."

But I kept on. "If a single bill is easy, how much is tough?"

She relented, grinned back in spite of the embarrassment. "They caught a girl last month with her vagina stuffed full."

"Of money?"

"Over two hundred dollars in twenties."

"What'd they do to the girl with the money liner?"

"They fired her."

"Uh huh. Who was bugging Juanita?"

"Had nothing to do with any of that. I never heard anything about Juanita trying to cheat the house. This was totally different."

"Who was it?"

"That cop."

"Which cop?"

"The young one that was tearing up my car."

"You're sure?"

She nodded her head. "Dead sure."

I winced. "Poor choice of words, Miss future Ph.D. Wish you hadn't put it just that way."

"You think I'm in danger?"

I knew damned well she was. I just wasn't sure why.

CHAPTER SEVEN

WE DRANK SOME COFFEE and Linda decided I needed some ice beneath the eye. She wrapped an ice cube in a paper napkin and was dabbing at the mouse with it. The napkin got soaked and started dripping onto my shirt, so she suggested I off with the shirt.

One thing led to another, there, and we ended up in the spa.

Like I've told you, I've been a cop most of my life. A cop usually finds himself living in the seams of life. I mean, we spend our days and nights involved in the lower depths. Gorgki. I'm no illiterate. What we have not experienced with people does not happen with people. We live with them all: murderers, rapists, psychos, thieves, con men, hookers, pimps, addicts, pornographers, screwed-up kids, mean-ass dudes, wife beaters, husband beaters, child abusers, parent abusers—we get them all, all the time. These are the people we live with.

But, you know, a cop has a different view of all this—different than the average citizen, I mean. Maybe it's the way news gets reported, but I think the average citizen tends to think in labels more than cops do. A murderer does nothing but go around murdering people; right? A hooker does nothing but screw people for a fee; right? From a distance, see, the criminal becomes the crime.

Not so, for a cop. We are dealing with these people as *people,* not as crimes. What they *do* is against the law. What they *are* is very human. And we have to deal with that. What I am trying to say is that these are the *people* of our world. As *people,* the murderer might be admirably devoted to his bedridden mother and the whore might spend all her afternoons at the old folks' home cheering up the residents. The child molester might be the leading philanthropist of the community and the shoplifter might be a loving wife and mother having trouble with menopause.

We're always hearing about brutal cops with anesthetized feelings and arrogance and how they're all cynics. Some, yeah; some get that way, or some start that way and get worse. But we're affected by our environment, just like everybody else. I guess that's why some cops go bad; why some cops who start bad go worse. We're subject, believe it or not, to the human condition, such as it is.

I have known cops who married hookers. Hookers they'd busted over and over again. End up marrying them. I have known cops who formed strong friendships with hardened criminals and went to bat for them, even visited them in prison or took care of their kids or whatever. We're *involved* in this world, see, and we're influenced by it, and we see these people as *people,* not as crimes.

All of which, I grant you, is a long way of saying that I was falling for Linda. Not that I put her in the class with any of those above. But, face it; she was living in the seams, too. Many people in our society—most people, I guess—would tend to judge her harshly for the way she makes a living. Any woman, they'd say, who romps around a stage bare-ass to incite lust in a gathering of men is really just a whore at heart. That's an extension of the label. A "whore at heart" is a whore indeed, in that line of thought.

I am here to tell you that Linda Shelton was not a whore to me, at heart or indeed. As between her and me—she, woman; me, man—the only remarkable difference about Linda lay in the person she was, not in what she did for a living.

And she was a delightful person.

She may have thrown off her clothes and thrown her muff into the faces of several hundred guys every night, but she slipped out of her clothes this time and into my spa with the same mix of timidity and uncertainty as any woman might show in similar circumstances. Which is to say she did not act the brazen slut. She did not act that way because she was not one.

I would almost have wished otherwise, at the moment. I am a direct person. I also have a direct sexuality. When a beautiful naked woman slips into the warm waters beside me, I have a very direct reaction —the kind my creator designed me for. And I stay that way until some sort of direct action brings me down. Not only do I stay that way, but the pressure to bring me down grows by quantum leaps and, by God, *demands* that something bring it down.

So, hell, I just grabbed her by the hips and hauled her over onto the lap.

In a muffled little voice she said, "Oh shit, Joe, don't do that."

I told her, "Every cell in my body is screaming at me to do that."

She said, "Dammit, so's mine—but let's not, huh? I mean, not like this."

"Like how, then?"

"Later. Okay? Please. Let's talk awhile first."

"Hell," I groaned. "We've been talking for hours. What do we talk about?"

She slid away, moved to the opposite side—the moving waters waving those marvelous tits at me—and said, "Let's talk about Joe. What makes him tick. What makes him mad, glad. You know. Introduce yourself first."

I said, "Oh, well, my favorite subject."

"Okay. Tell me."

I said, "Suddenly my mind's a total blank. Barely remember my name."

"It's Joe. Joe Copp. Remember now? Who is he?"

"Copp for hire, yeah." Right now, he is ninety-nine percent..." I let my eyes finish the statement.

She giggled. "Another theory exploded."

"What theory is that?"

She said, "Has to do with strong men and—you know."

I sighed. "Maybe it's all relative."

"Not in your case," she said. "Dammit, Joe. No wonder you scare your women."

"That's not what I meant and you know it. Anyway, there's nothing here to scare anybody."

Those eyes gleamed wickedly. "It could be an interesting investigation, I guess."

"I'm interested," I assured her.

"Me, too. But I have some scruples about these things. I don't lay with a man I know nothing about."

"Didn't ask you to lay."

"Okay. I don't sit on their flagpoles, either."

It became a laugher.

"Born in Palo Alto," I told her.

"Oh, very good. I love Palo Alto."

"I didn't. Stodgy and dull. Nobody's sweat even smells there."

"So where did you go?"

"San Jose."

"Gritty."

"You bet. Everything smells in San Jose."

"Just your cup of tea, then. What happened there?"

"Forgot myself, one day. Had a little rhubarb with the chief, knocked him on his ass."

"It seemed wise to leave after that."

"Seemed wise, yeah. Went to San Francisco."

"Even grittier than San Jose."

"Oh. Say. Much more. You haven't smelled life at all until you've smelled it in San Francisco."

"What happened there?"

"Come back over here and I'll tell you."

"Tell me right where I'm at, Samson."

"Let you cut my hair."

"Darn! Forgot and left my chainsaw at home."

"I bleed like other men."

"Sure, but you've got more to spare."

I said, "See? I *do* intimidate you."

She said, "Of course you do. What happened in San Francisco?"

"Replay of San Jose. But with the mayor."

"Wow. You don't fool around."

"He was an asshole."

"The way I hear it, most mayors are."

"Yeah, but this one used his for politics, I think."

"You couldn't tolerate that."

"Not usually."

She laughed and I laughed.

Then she came back to me and climbed aboard. Not altogether aboard but close.

"I really like you," I told her.

"Think I kind of like you too," she told me.

"Raise up," I suggested. "And come just a little closer."

"How do you do this?"

"This what? Surely you know how to do this."

"Not that. *This.*" She nudged me. *"That.* How do you keep it there like that for so long?"

I assured her, "It keeps itself. Come on. Up and over. We'll see how well it keeps itself under the gun."

She said, "Huh uh. So far we're still in San Francisco—"

We were not destined to get any farther than San Francisco this time.

The picture window about ten feet to our right exploded inward. It's one-way glass—I can see out but others cannot see in without really working at it—and we were in muted lighting, so I guess the guy was firing blindly and trusting to luck, but somebody just beyond that shattered glass was pumping buckshot into the room in a murderous fire pattern via a semiautomatic shotgun.

Stuff was flying everywhere and moving our way by

the time my reactions took hold. I pulled Linda to the bottom of the tub with me and held her there until she began to fight me, then gave us nose depth and no more until I could assure myself that it was reasonably prudent to expose more.

I charged up out of there then with a mad like I had not tasted for a long time, grabbed a pistol from a drawer of the desk and quietly went out the back door.

Caught a glimpse of the guy in time to get off a couple of rounds as he disappeared at the corner of the house—but it was only a glimpse and I knew better than to chase after him.

I was, after all, balls naked and dripping wet.

But I was alive and Linda was alive.

I figured we got lucky. And I felt like the biggest jerk in town.

I should have been expecting something like that. Somebody was on a killing streak, and it was not just for kicks.

Jerk, yeah. I'd damned near got the lady killed. It was time to stop being a jerk. It was time, maybe, to start giving back.

CHAPTER EIGHT

I GUESS MORE THAN ANYTHING ELSE I was fuming over the loose way I'd been playing the thing, like it was some kind of game and I was having fun with it, in spite of the deaths of three people in a matter of hours. In defense of my stupidity, though, let me point out that I'd gotten into the thing sort of edgewise. If I'd been a public cop I'd still be working on my reports. A lot had gone down in a very short time. There had not even been time enough for me to start having a good theory about the case.

With Juanita in the early going, I had been sort of halfway inclining toward spurned lover or fruitcake. I figured she hadn't come entirely clean with me and that the hidden facts would emerge on their own with even a shallow investigation. If she'd been stalked, raped and killed in a sex crime, that would have been a case with a familiar color. To be run down by a car, though, moments after consulting a private investigator for help, suggested a totally different sort of motive for murder. Also, early on there, I could not even entirely rule out a purely accidental death. After all, the girl had not come to me asking that I save her life. A guy was bugging her—or that was the story—and she wanted him bugged-off; no big deal.

Before I could even begin to assimilate those ideas, I go and find her roommate murdered beyond any doubt. This could have been a sex crime, though, with no relation to the first death; all the marks were there. Even the torture angle. But a sex killer does not usually tear the scene apart in a search of the premises. Looking at the whole picture there, it would seem that the murder was almost incidental to something else. The torture and the frantic search of the premises pointed to that "something else." But that was all I really had, at this point.

Then I have my little run-in with Tanner and Jones; they both seem more interested in what I know about Juanita than in what happened to Juanita. During the two hours I have been away someone has ransacked my office in a way strongly similar to the scene at Juanita's apartment. Is it coincidence that I find Tanner and Jones waiting for me there? Is it also coincidence that Tanner logged himself onto the case before he was even officially on duty? And wasn't it just a bit too sloppy, even for Tanner, to let the traffic detail conduct the only official investigation at the scene? Sure it was; but again and still, all I had were deep rumbles and a what-the-hell.

So I go to talk to George the bartender for a bit of insight. He gives me a "could-be" ID of Juanita's pest as a reserve cop but the situation is a bit too tense at this point to question George in fine detail. He has given me further reason to wonder about Ed Jones, though, and while I am off trying to learn more about Jones I learn also that Jones' partner and mentor apparently has some private police arrangement with the management at the New Frontier, which joint appears to be at the eye of this storm. Tanner and Jones have apparently responded privately to a trouble call brought on by my visit to that establishment; while there, then, George the bartender becomes the third fatality in this rapidly developing case—I'm still cop enough to fall into such bullshit jargon—which began so innocuously several hours earlier. Then a girl who I'd seen earlier as the bewitching and bare-ass Belinda on the stage at New Frontier enters my vehicle—cops have "vehicles," never "cars"—and urgently requests that I get her the hell out and gone from there. Ed Jones has apparently "found" in her car the gun that killed George the bartender.

Now I am already in violation of my license. I have failed to report a capital crime; I have withheld information concerning another one; I have destroyed private property and improperly intimidated citizens during the course of an investigation.

So I figure what the hell and take it a step farther; I directly interfere with a murder investigation by spiriting away the prime suspect of the moment.

Which is about where I was at, in the spa with Linda before the gunplay began. In the case, that is where I was at. In my head, I was nowhere in the case. Linda had fingered Ed Jones as definitely the guy who had been bugging Juanita Valdez. That did not necessarily mean that Jones had anything to do with the death of Juanita, or any of the other stuff. I had no ID whatever linking Jones to the death car. But at that moment when gunfire shattered the window of my bedroom, none of that was at the surface of my mind.

I'd had only one thing on my mind at the time, and that was why I felt such a jerk.

I had damn near got the girl killed... over my hankering for a piece of tail.

And, yeah, that rankled; it really burned, deep down. So I guess that feeling had a lot to do with the way I reacted to the incident.

Linda was still sputtering and gasping in the spa when I came back from the yard and hauled her out of there. I toweled her down and commanded her to get dressed while I did the same for myself. This time I installed the hardware in a shoulder holster; I am licensed to carry, of course, and I would have been an idiot to do otherwise, even without the license. I was finally starting to think, and the thoughts were not pleasant.

So we were out of there within five minutes of the attack. I wanted to drop the lady into a safe stash and then I wanted to invade this case in at least a semi-intelligent fashion.

I have a scanner in the car. I turned it on and punched up the local police channels just to keep an ear on my world, then told my passenger, who had uttered not a word since the shooting, "I need a live client. Tell me I'm hired."

She stirred beside me; muttered, "Hired for what?"

"Hired to keep you alive. It's a technicality. Don't worry the fee. I'll make it a dollar a day. Just tell me I'm hired."

She asked in a muffled voice, "Why would anyone want to kill me?"

"Funny, I was about to ask you the same question."

She shook her head. "I figured they were after you."

"Maybe," I said, "and maybe not. And maybe both of us. Do you own a gun?"

She made a face. "Absolutely not. And don't even suggest to me that I should carry one."

"Not suggesting that," I told her. "Just wondering how good the frame."

"What frame?"

I said, "The cop claims to have found the death weapon in your car. You claim that George was shot by someone as he walked away from your car. So—"

"What do you mean, I *claim.*"

"Just telling it like it seems, kid. It's your word against the cop's, and that could get very sticky. Especially if the gun turns out to be directly connected to you before the fact."

"That's ridiculous. I have never so much as *touched* a gun in my whole life. *Hate* the damned things."

"Simmer down," I said. "Just trying to cover the bases here. Why were you and George sitting outside in your car?"

"Well, we for sure weren't necking."

"So why outside instead of inside?"

"He followed me out. I left early. You tore the place up—*remember*? Then those cops came, and I guess most of the customers had already decided it was not a good night to hang around. The place was nearly empty. So I left. George came out to see if I was okay. That's all."

"So you sat there talking about how okay you were."

"No, we sat there talking about Juanita and what kind of trouble she'd been in."

"So what kind of trouble was it?"

"Well, it got her killed, didn't it?"

"Looks that way, yeah. Got George killed too, maybe. And almost you. So what kind of trouble?"

"God, Joe, I don't know. I just know that George was very upset. He wanted to talk about Juanita. Wanted to talk about *you* and your interest in all this."

"So what was the verdict on all that?"

"I don't know what you mean. There was no *verdict*. We just knew that Juanita was in some sort of trouble and we'd been trying to help her, that's all. Now it was too late to help her, and we were wondering what it was all about."

"George was wondering that?"

"Yes. Me, too. George told me he'd figured it out, he thought—that she was into something heavy and the cops were watching her. He was puzzled by your interest in the thing. I told him I'd recommended you to Juanita. I hadn't known about this police angle. I just knew—or I was told by Juanita—that some creep was following her around and she didn't want to go to the police with it."

"So how'd you know about me?"

She moved to the far side of the seat. I felt her eyes on me for a long moment but I was busy driving so couldn't try to read anything there. Finally she told me, "I've started work on my doctoral thesis."

"That's nice," I said "Good luck with it. Hope you live to see it through."

She said, "Don't do that to me, Joe."

"Do what?"

"You're pulling away from me. Please don't. I'm scared to death. Please help me."

I said, "Tell me I'm hired."

"You're *hired*, damn it."

"And stop evading my questions. How the hell can I help blindfolded?"

"I wasn't evading. I was explaining. My thesis, among other things, investigates the influence of names on personality. One particularly intriguing influence has to do with the selection of careers. Is it pure coincidence that a man with a name like *Shears* is a hair stylist? Or that Dr. Yankum is a dentist, Dr. Corona is an eye surgeon, Jack Hammer is a construction worker and Bill Drains is a plumber?"

"I knew a hooker once," I said, "named, for real, Harriet Ball."

"Great. I'll add her to my list. That's how I found you. Someone told me about this hardboiled cop with the, to him, I guessed, highly suggestive name of *Joe Copp*. By the time I tracked you down, you were *Copp for Hire*. There's a doubling here, too. You see, *Joe* is a strength name. Men named Joe are usually very assertive and commanding. Team that with Copp and I figured a good combination for Juanita's problem."

"You read tea leaves and cast horoscopes too?"

"That's easy. You're a Leo. Enough said."

I could not just leave it at that. "Suppose you're a Pisces. Swim both ways at once. What does *Linda* versus *Belinda* tell me?"

She moved back close. "*Belinda* is the root name. It's Germanic, not Spanish as you would think. The Spanish *Linda* means *pretty.*"

"What does Belinda mean?"

"Originally, a serpent."

"No kidding."

"It was the title of an oracular priestess. *Linda* is a diminutive."

"You don't look much like a serpent to me," I said. "Especially not on stage."

"You're forgetting Eden. The serpent is mankind's oldest symbol of temptation."

It was a symbol for something else, too.

But actually I don't put that much stock in names, Copp notwithstanding. And I really did not want to think about snakes.

Besides... we had a tail. And it was crowding closer and closer as we sped down the mountainside.

CHAPTER NINE

IF YOU MEAN TO PLAY vehicular games on a winding mountain road at night, you should know the territory better than your opponent knows it.

I had been driving that road for five years, at all times of the day and night.

This guy had come to play games.

It was his tough luck that he had come to play in my territory.

He was crowding my rear bumper close enough that I could see the orange flames decaled across the hood in my rearview. I sent Linda a warning signal with the eyes and told her to buckle up.

She obeyed quickly. Linda was no dummy. She knew what was coming down, even before the guy rode up and tapped my bumper.

I drive an old Cadillac, one that was built before the EPA standards scaled them down to economy size. Sumbitch weighs three tons, believe it or not, and packs five-hundred cubic inches beneath the hood. It's like an armored tank, and that's why I love it so, even when the monthly gas bill comes.

So I was not going to let that TransAm push me off the road.

In fact, I damned well dared him to try. Next time he surged forward for the tap, I tapped my brakes. The tap became a cruncher and sent him swerving away in reaction. He lost a headlight in that exchange but not a lot of nerve because he came right back for more, this time nosing up past my rear end on the passing side.

Bad timing on that one, though. Another vehicle swept around a curve headed our way about a hundred feet ahead, sending the guy swerving back in line. Even with that, he tried to clip me as he swung back in, caught maybe a silly millimeter of bumper, which affected him more than it did me.

By the time he was in control again we were riding the final ridge before the road curved abruptly into a descent to level terrain. It was about a three-hundred-foot drop graded over maybe a quarter of a mile if you stayed on the road; if you didn't it was just about foot for foot on the descent—not the way you want to do it in a vehicle.

There was a turnout at the curve, a widening of the

shoulder to allow a park-and-view of the valley below. It was on the uphill side. I went for it, with the Trans-Am again crowding the rear.

I did not go all the way.

He did.

Maybe because he was so intent on me, maybe because of the limited visibility resulting from the smashed headlight; maybe because he was a jerk and had been trying for three miles to buy something like this.

Anyway, I did a sliding Uey with the Cad; he tried too late to do the same with the TransAm. It teetered broadside at the edge, then went on over in a slowly rolling descent.

I sprang a backup .25 automatic from the glove box and dropped it on Linda's lap, hate them or not, and bailed out of there with my big piece leading the way.

One of the nice things about being a big man is that it enables you to pack a big piece without unnecessarily advertising the fact that you're carrying. Not that I ever considered it necessary to carry a cannon. Most of the shooting I've ever done was on a pistol range. That's true of most cops. You have to fill out too damned many forms if you fire your weapon in the line of duty. But there is a psychological advantage to a big piece if you are in a stare-down with some dude holding a little snubnosed pocket piece. So years ago I adopted a Smith & Wesson Model 57 double-action revolver. It's a 41 Magnum, which is a bit unusual; has an 8–3/8″ barrel, more than a foot long overall and weighs over four pounds loaded. Theatrical as hell, I know; but then half of what a cop does is theatrical, so what the hell. If I can prevent a shooting just by unbuttoning my jacket, why not? But if it does get to a shooting, the S&W 57 is very accurate and reloads quickly.

I had a shooting now. My boy had ridden the wreck all the way, I guess. I went scrambling down the hill behind him and drew fire about halfway down. I sent two quick rounds sizzling into the wreckage and got no answer. But I had to respect the return-fire capability, so that slowed me. By the time I got down there my boy was gone. I found some blood on the front seat and a smear on a rock just outside the car, and that was as close as I got to the guy.

I jotted down the license number and took the pertinent info off the registration, which I found in the glove box. Registered to a guy who lived in La Canada, which is the other side of Pasadena. Had no doubt at all that the vehicle would show up on the stolen-car list.

Linda was waiting for me all a'sweat outside the Cad when I finally got back topside. I noticed that she did not have the little pistol I'd dropped on her.

"Where's your gun?"

She pointed to the car, then nearly fainted in my arms. I provided physical support but I was fuming.

"Wouldn't have done you much good, would it," I groused, "if the wrong guy had come back up that hill."

She did not reply to that but only clung closer. I gave her time to get it back together, then disentangled and led her to the car.

Neither of us had a lot to say about anything at all. So it was a pretty quiet ride the rest of the way. I took her to a luxury hotel in Covina and checked us in with fictitious names. That's only a misdemeanor offense so my crimes were getting lighter. I did not want to advertise her presence anywhere, not even in Covina, which is another jurisdiction. In case someone might go searching, I figured the classy joint would be among the last places to look. It was built entirely around interior courtyards and every room was a suite with kitchen capabilities, so it could also be a comfortable place to lie low for a while, if that should be necessary.

I tucked her into the suite and went looking for provisions, first making sure that she understood she was not to open the door to anyone but me. Cops or anyone else; let them kick their way inside if it should come to that.

I found a twenty-four-hour mart just a few minutes away; bought instant coffee and milk, some fruits and a few snack foods; also filled a requisition from Linda for cosmetic necessities.

She was wrapped in a towel when she let me back into the suite, and I noticed the phone was off the hook. "Why the phone?"

"I'm talking to my mother. Please be quiet."

Be quiet, my ass.

I went over and picked it up, covered the transmitter with my hand. "No goddamned phone calls, Linda."

She said, "Don't be silly. I always call her when I get home from work. She would be worried silly. I didn't tell her what's going on."

"You don't tell her where you're at," I said, properly contrite.

"Of course not."

I gave her the phone and she quickly ended the conversation. Didn't even know she had a mother. How was I supposed to know who she was talking to?

I put the perishable stuff in the refrigerator and took the cosmetics to the bathroom.

She was staring at the phone when I returned to the sitting room.

I said, "Sorry 'bout that, kid."

She said, "It's okay. I understand. You're worried for me."

"Worried as hell, that's right. There have been two attempts on your life in the past hour. So..."

She shivered. "Why do you think?"

"Hell, I don't know what to think. Unless Juanita was into some very hard trouble and the people who are mad at her think you might know something about it. Do you?"

She gave me a blank look. "I don't know anything about it."

"Maybe you do but don't know that you do."

"What could it be?"

I said, "Anything, just anything."

"Well, I don't know how to account for just anything, Joe."

I growled, "Neither do I. Was Juanita screwing around with extracurricular stuff?"

"You mean, literally screwing around?"

"Professionally, yeah."

She shook her head. "I don't know, Joe. Some of the girls are in business for themselves, but I never saw anything to make me think that Juanita was. That doesn't mean that she could not or did not make dates. I think she was the type to weigh the pros and cons of any offer. It would be entirely a matter of practicality for Juanita. I do believe, though, that she was very careful about her involvements."

"What about her roommate? Know her?"

"I've met her."

"So?"

"So her name is Maria Avila. She tried out for the club about a year ago. Oh, I guess she tried several times. I don't know—something's lacking in Maria. Pretty as a picture and a fair dancer but . . . I don't know, no pizazz, I guess. Juanita told me that she'd made a connection with one of the party agencies. You know, private parties."

"Sometimes *very* private parties?"

"I suppose. Some of these agencies are straight and some are not. Some will book a party or whatever."

"Whatever covers a lot."

"Covers everything," she said simply. "I believe Maria does everything."

"What if I told you," I said, thinking about it and wondering if I should, "that Maria is dead too?"

She blinked. "Is she?"

I decided against all the cards face up, said instead, "I said what if. Why would you think she is dead?"

She looked at me through clouded eyes. "I would figure she finally took that step too far."

Step too far. Well. Maybe so. Maybe she and Juanita had taken it together. And it was now catching up to Linda and me.

I had to do something quickly to halt the fall of dominoes.

Sudden death, after all, had already knocked twice at our door. I did not want to be standing around dumb and defenseless when it came again.

CHAPTER TEN

I HAVE A FRIEND AT COUNTY, a true friend. Her name is Edna Sorensen. She is about five feet tall and five feet around, fiftyish, and I am in love with her. Edna is one of the most thoroughly nice people I have ever known.

Her kid got into the drug scene a few years back. Nice kid but too impressionable at an impressionable age. She discovered privately that he was dealing coke to his friends at school in order to support his own expensive habit.

I was with the department then and she came to me for advice. I took the kid in hand and helped him straighten himself out. He's now in his third year at UCLA and it looks like he'll be graduating with honors.

Edna and I have been friends ever since. I see her

rarely since I left the department, but a week does not go by without her calling and chatting. Also a chat does not go by without her reminding me of her gratitude for the thing with the kid.

Well, I actually did not do all that much, and I never considered what I did do as a quid pro quo. Edna owes me nothing and I had yet to ask a favor of her.

But I did badly need a friend at this point and I needed one with Edna's encyclopedic knowledge of people and events at County. She's a supervisor in the personnel division, and what she doesn't know has not been recorded.

So I went calling on Edna at twenty minutes past midnight on that Thursday morning. I know her husband Nils only very slightly; he works for the county, too, but in the parks department. Nice man, soft-spoken, a bit old-worldly. Got them both out of bed and both seemed honored that I had done so.

Nils put on the coffee while I went through the preliminaries with his wife at the kitchen table.

I told her, "I don't want you to tell me anything that would compromise you."

She replied, "I understand perfectly."

I told her, "I'm like fighting in the dark without a flashlight."

She said, "I understand. You need a light."

"That is exactly what I need, Edna. But not at your expense. Tell me that you understand that."

"I understand that, Joe. How can I help you?"

"A newly made detective named Ed Jones came over from the reserves recently. He's now riding shotgun for Gil Tanner, San Gabriel Division. I need a make on this guy."

She pursed her lips, looked at her husband, then told me, "I know that one. He has PI."

"PI meaning political influence."

"Who is his sponsor?"

She again looked at her husband before saying, "Jim Davitsky."

Davitsky is one of our more colorful county supervisors. Very rich, very powerful even before his election to the board several years ago. People are always asking, "What does Jim need with the county?" Jim's answer to that, of course, is that the county needs him. He dines at the White House, this guy. I think he has an eye on Sacramento and the governor's mansion—and maybe beyond.

I took a moment to digest that bit of news, then asked Edna, "What's the connection between Jones and Davitsky?"

"Jim is his uncle," she said without bothering to check it with her husband.

"I see." I saw, indeed. "Anything improper about Jones's appointment?"

She looked to her husband for a long moment.

He told her, very quietly, "Coffee in a minute, dear. Give the man what he needs."

She turned back to me, fidgeted with the plastic tablecloth for a moment, sighed and told me, "I think it was improper influence, yes. Ed Jones has a cloud in his past. Another man with his record would not be with the department."

"What's that cloud, Edna?"

She shook her head. "Don't know for sure. Something to do with army service. He was with the military police in Germany. An administrative review board turned him down when he first applied for the reserve program. That review is confidential and sealed. It would take a court order to open it. But then he applied again a few months later and this time sailed through without a scratch. Then the military record came up again over his activation to full-duty status. I remember there was quite a row but I don't know all the details of that. I do know that Jim Davitsky personally intervened that time and the activation went through."

Nils brought the coffee over and poured us each a cup. Ever drink Scandinavian coffee? You can chew it. I chewed mine and asked Edna, "What do you know about Gil Tanner?"

She made a face, flipped her coffeecup with a finger. "He's a bad cop, Joe."

"I know that from personal observation, but how do you know?"

"You should see his service record. No, on second thought, maybe you shouldn't. It would make a good cop like you throw up."

"Thanks for the vote but I need more than that if you can feed me."

She sighed again. "I don't recall all the details. But I can tell you that he has been charged with everything from brutality to dereliction of duty—and right now he's being reviewed on a gross misuse of office."

I looked at Nils, looked at her. "And what would that be?"

"Apparently he and some other detectives have formed a private company to provide industrial security services on the moonlight. It smells almost like a protection racket. They offer you their services but you don't need them. Very quick after you turn them down you suddenly need the services. The record suggests everything from fire bombings to burglary."

"That's pretty gross, yeah."

She added, "And one complainant was pistol-whipped by a masked intruder during a break-in. The man had refused their services that very day."

"How big is this, Edna?"

"Not too big right now, I guess. Seems to be centered mostly in your area at this time—"

"But it's under investigation?"

She nodded. "Tanner's group has been ordered to produce the records on all their accounts."

"Have you seen those records?"

"They haven't been produced yet. They claimed computer malfunction and requested a thirty-day stay."

I sat there and chewed coffee for a moment, then asked her, "Anything else?"

"Isn't that enough?"

"Ever hear anything about a joint in county jurisdiction called the New Frontier?"

She said, "Don't think so. What kind of joint?"

"Strip joint."

"Oh. One of those. I do vaguely remember something... not the name but the kind... something a few months ago involving Jim Davitsky and a strip joint."

"Bingo. What do you remember about that?"

"That's all... gossip, I think... something about Davitsky and his hidden interest in these strip joints. I think it was several of them."

"Sounds farfetched, doesn't it. Why would a guy like Davitsky get involved in something like that? Not for the money..."

Nils gave me a solemn wink. "Some men aren't always ruled by their pocketbooks."

"Very profound, Nils. What rules in place of money?"

"Vanity, power, love, sex. Not necessarily in that order."

Wisdom from the garden.

I said, "Bingo again. So which one of those, do you figure, would take a guy with high political aspirations into an involvement with strip joints?"

He replied in his quietly droll manner, "Surely not love."

Surely not. No. So that left vanity, power, and sex. With some men those three were interchangeable. And either one could produce murderous intent.

So what the hell did I have here now?

I had all three, pal. I had it all.

CHAPTER ELEVEN

THE FRAMING SPLINTERED AWAY and the whole thing fell in under a single kick. I walked across the fallen door with the S&W leading the way and caught Tanner in his underwear in front of the TV, a beer in one hand and a cigar in the other, gawking at me in disbelief with his gunleather just out of reach on the floor beside him.

I kicked the hardware rig across the room and holstered my own piece, then took his cigar and his beer away from nonresistant hands and tossed both into the fireplace. I turned off the television; pointed a finger at him. "Stay!"—and went to check out the rest of the apartment. It was a small condo with a very cramped living room—hardly more than a wide hallway leading off to the kitchen and dining nook—one bedroom, one bath.

If a man's home is his castle, Gil Tanner was a monk. Except that I found a girl in the monk's bath. She'd just emerged from the shower—probably hastily, after hearing the commotion—and was reaching for a towel as I pushed the door open.

She froze; gave me a stunned look and nothing else.

I handed her the towel and nothing else, went back to the living room.

Tanner was being a good boy. Hadn't budged from the chair.

He was shitface scared. I stood over him. "Now we talk."

He swallowed around a lump in the throat and asked, "What is this, Joe?"

"It's the end of it," I told him.

"End of what, Joe?"

"Today you resign."

"From the department? Joe! That's crazy! I'm sixteen months from retirement—"

"You didn't earn it, Tanner. Today you resign. And you tell Davitsky no more killings."

That appeared to do the trick.

"What?"

"Your little creep partner, too. Tell *him* no more killings. If you want a good reason for doing that, just keep this in mind—you will be the second to die. Right after him. Understand that? It's not a threat; it's a commitment."

I showed him my back and went to the shattered

doorway. "What do you do with all your loot, Tanner? You live like pigs."

He did not respond; just gave me a glassy look.

I went on out and along the hall; encountered an old man in a security uniform who was just entering the building.

I smiled at him and he asked me. "What's all the disturbance?"

I told him, "Wild party back there, I guess. Naked women and all."

He muttered, "We'll by God see about that," and hurried on.

I went out to my car, took time to light a cigarette and wonder if anything had been accomplished, then took off. I had another stop not far away and wanted to get there ahead of my advertisements.

It was in one of the new townhouse developments just off Baseline. Very stylish and "in" with junior executives. Which includes, I guess, pizza parlor managers and young entrepreneurs cum deputy sheriffs such as Ed Jones. The "young family" evidence was everywhere, various types of wheeled toys scattered about. Not the sort of place where you'd like to introduce gunplay of any kind.

The one I was looking for had lighted windows; it was the only one around that did. Drapes were drawn so I could see nothing of the interior. But I could hear the murmur of a television late-night movie through the front door; sounded close to the door. I pushed the bell button and got a response about two beats later, as though someone had been standing just inside waiting for that very thing.

A peephole opened, an eye was there, and a woman's voice inquired, "Yes?" It sounded more like a *ya* than a *yes*, definitely accented.

I asked the peephole, "Is Ed home?"

The voice replied, "Who asks?"

I told it, "I'm Joe Copp. Working with Ed on a case. Has he come home yet?"

There was a brief hesitation. I could almost hear the woman's mind clicking along its gears. Then I heard the bolt move and the door inched open to reveal an intact safety chain and a two-inch-wide view of a young woman with a very unhappy face. She was wearing a bathrobe, and she was either fat or pregnant.

I voted for pregnant and told her, "Nothing to worry. Sorry to bother you. Can I leave a message?"

"You are working with Ed?"

I replied, "Sort of, yes."

"He should be home one hour ago. Do you work long with Ed?"

I was getting a drift and decided to play it. "A while, yeah. Can I leave the message?"

"Do you work the twelve-hour shift, too?"

I said, "Not usually."

This kid was very agitated. She said, "What means not usually? Sometimes yes, sometimes no?"

I had the drift, yeah. I told her, "Well, you know a cop's work. It's never done. Okay if I come in just for a minute? I'd like to leave a message."

The door closed abruptly in my face. I heard the chain rattle, then the door opened again, wide.

Pretty kid. Very blond, very Nordic... and yeah, very pregnant. I guessed ninth month and ready to pop at any moment. Hell, it was two o'clock in the morning. This kid should have been getting her sleep, not tending the latch for a wandering husband. A Japanese monster movie was on the tube. A basket of knitting thread sat on the couch; she'd been building something for the baby, a nest outside for the grand opening.

I told her, and meant it, "I'm really sorry to bother you," as I moved inside.

She closed the door and turned to me with a tired smile. "It is okay. It is lonely. I do not mind. Are you still at work?"

I said yes because I felt for the kid, decided not to play a game. She brightened a bit at that, deciding maybe that if I were still at work, maybe her husband was too.

I told her, "Things have been rough lately. It will calm down soon." I gently touched the belly. "In time for junior, maybe. How much longer?"

She rubbed it. "Soon now. Do you need pad?"

I produced my own notebook and pen as I told her, "Thanks, no. Do you miss Germany?"

She showed me a smile. "Yes. But here is beautiful, this California. I will get accustomed—used."

She'd already been used but I didn't want to tell her that. I had the pen in position at the pad when I casually inquired, "Was Ed with the MPs when you guys got married?"

"Yes," she replied. "We are married now two years."

I said, "Beautiful. And baby makes three."

She smiled. "Yes. Baby makes all things better."

I hoped so, but figured not. "Raw deal he got, huh? I mean, you know, the trouble in Germany."

She said, "Yes."

I said, "I never got the straight of that."

She said, "Ed does not like to speak of it. One day he will tell you maybe."

I said, "Yeah," and jotted my note, tore it out, handed it to her.

She read it. "What means *Learn to drive?*"

I told her, "Ed will understand. Just please see that he gets it the minute he comes home. Okay?"

She smiled brightly. "Okay. You did not put your name."

"He'll know that too. Why don't you go to bed? Ed could be quite late tonight."

"Oh, I do not mind." She looked at the knitting.

"A baby makes all things better," I reminded her, feeling like a two-faced ass as I said it.

It would take more than a baby, I knew, to straighten out a guy like Ed Jones.

It might even take a bullet.

I hoped not as I bade the young lady goodnight.

It was not a good night.

But, by God, it was getting better all the time.

CHAPTER TWELVE

DIFFERENT PEOPLE go into police work for different reasons. Some come into it with a lot of idealism; think they can make a difference in an indifferent world. I know I felt that way. But the thing that really tipped me into it instead of into some other line of work was my love for a man who unofficially took me under his wing when I was ten years old.

My dad was killed in an automobile accident. My mom took over as provider and I became a latchkey kid. Guess I could have gone any way, at that time. But Hank Greer was a neighbor and he was a cop. Had three daughters, no son. Hank was the kind of man who needs a son, and there I was in need, like they say, of a male role model.

He took me fishing and hunting and got me interested in sports. I idolized the man. My mom started going a little haywire when I was in junior high, started hanging out in bars and bringing home a constantly changing lineup of jerks to sleep with. Don't hold that against her, now; she had no bed of roses, and I guess you reach for what's there when the desperation gets to you. Of course I didn't have that kind of understanding at the time, and it bothered me all to hell.

Well, the less she mothered the more Hank fathered. I moved in with his family when I was sixteen. Don't know to this day whatever became of my mom. She just sort of drifted away. I think maybe she finally died of her broken heart, but I've never really tried to find out. Probably afraid of the truth.

Anyway, things were fine with my surrogate family. I played big brother to the girls, an oversized eager puppy to the mother, and a good buddy to the father. Made all-state linebacker my last two years in high school and was offered scholarships at Cal and Stanford. Turned them down, and that made Hank sick. But I wanted to be like him, and I couldn't see waiting through four years of college to start.

So I enrolled in a local junior college and took courses in criminology and police procedures, aiming toward the police academy. Got there, too, soon as I met the age requirement.

One week after my graduation from the Police Academy Hank was killed in a shootout during a drug bust. It came out a short while later that he had been criminally involved with the guy who killed him. That hurt, yeah. Hurt like hell. I wouldn't buy it until the facts were simply too plain to buy anything else. But I was not downed by that. I think it just firmed up my own resolve to be the best damned cop in town—and I knew what a good cop was *supposed* to be.

It has put me through a lot of trouble, though, that ideal. And I finally just gave it up, but not the way some guys do. I mean, I did not give in to the system. I moved outside the system and tried to become the best damned private cop in town. Not that it is all that impossible to be a good cop within the system. Many guys make it through just fine. It's a matter of timing, circumstance and personality. Mine all seemed to be wrong most of the time. I was a square peg in a round hole, and that was uncomfortable all the way.

But I do know a lot of guys who are fine cops doing a fine job of law enforcement, and there's nobody hanging all over their backs while they're doing it. I think maybe my problem is that I'm just too damn visible. You can't look the other way when I am headed your way. Which makes for confrontations, and I mostly seem to come down on the unpopular side of an issue.

So maybe I'm a jerk.

I am a jerk. I could be making a bundle if I just

hired myself out to anybody for anything. But, see, I never started out to make a bundle. I'm content to make a living, with my principles, such as they are, intact.

I started out to talk about the reasons why people go into police work. I gave you one, idealism, and believe it or not a lot of people can be counted in that group. Some, though, go into it strictly as a practical matter. Beats pumping gas or running a delivery route. Pay has gotten quite respectable, too, plus all the health and pension benefits. Besides all that, there's a certain dignity to being a cop. Guys who go into it for practical reasons can go any of three ways: they can be good cops, or bad or so-so. Many in this class are just so-so. Some others go into it because they have this idea that it's exciting and glamorous work. They usually don't stay with it, but those who do stay come down to earth damned quick, and some develop into damned fine cops.

But there's another class of cop that I am getting at here.

This guy is a natural asshole. He is not worth much of a shit for anything because he is essentially a bad ass and would be behind bars except for the badge. This guy is a natural bully, and a natural bully is really a cowardly asshole looking for easy victims to elevate his own putrid image of himself. This guy would have been one of Hitler's early brownshirts and later a concentration-camp commando. You would never find him leading troops into combat, because combat is dangerous and this asshole is not looking for dangerous honors, he is looking for easy victories.

If you should meet up with this asshole wearing a badge, look out. He will cut you down to his own size in any way he can, and he wears the badge solely as a means of doing just that.

They look for guys like this during the screening of police candidates, but somehow a few always manage to slip through. Some of them manage to evade official detection for a hell of a long time—sometimes for an entire police career—and some of them even reach high rank. Then you've really got a problem, and I have had those kinds of problems.

One of these guys in a department is bad news enough. Several are scary. Get them together as a team and you've got yourself a full-blown nightmare.

So what I am trying to tell you is that we had ourselves a full-blown nightmare in the San Gabriel Valley.

I was not certain at this point just how strongly the nightmare figured in my particular problems of the moment, but I felt sure it was there.

I needed to find out just how much it figured. And I intended to find out very damned quick.

It was a small office suite in an industrial complex housing also a number of hi-tech outfits and various service facilities numbering maybe a hundred different companies.

The decal on the door read: *SecurityMasters Unlimited.*

The lights were on and I could see a guy seated behind a desk as I drove by. A van parked directly in front bore the same decal as the one on the office door.

I parked a bit up-range and watched the door for ten minutes.

Nothing went in or out. It was almost three o'clock. Only one other company in the complex was showing any signs of activity at that moment, a computer outfit that was receiving merchandise at a small loading dock at the far side.

I left the car and gave the area a quick feel on foot, then went calling on *SecurityMasters.*

The glass door was locked.

I rapped on it, and the guy looked up from the desk. He seemed a bit bored, more than a bit sleepy.

I opened my coat and let him get a look at the hardware as I placed my ID wallet against the glass.

He hurriedly stumbled to his feet and came over, unlocked the door without even a glance at the ID and swung it open. Which was dumb.

I moved with the door and pushed it into his face.

He went down without a sound and made no move to get back up. I walked around him on my way to the desk, pulled out all the drawers and dropped everything onto the floor. Not looking for anything in particular; just titting for tat.

The door to an inner office was locked. I kicked it open. Actually there were two offices back there, connected by a narrow hallway. Each contained a desk and a filing cabinet. Everything was locked up.

I went out and checked the guy on the floor. He was still out. I found no keys on him but I did find a wallet with forty bucks and a reserve deputy ID. I left it lying on his chest and went out to the car, brought back a tire tool, went to work on the locks in the inner offices.

They popped open with hardly any leverage at all.

And, yeah, I found some goodies back there.

Not spectacular goodies but good-enough goodies.

Good enough to maybe put the whole rotten operation out of business for good.

I wrote a note and folded it into the unconscious guy's hand, then gathered up my goodies and went away.

All the note said was: "SecurityMasters, my ass." And I knew I didn't need to sign it.

I was going to have those guys all over my back before the sun rose.

I hoped so, anyway.

CHAPTER THIRTEEN

I WAS GETTING THE FEELING that I was involved in two separate and distinct problems here—or else two problems with tenuous linkage between them.

I could not shake from my mind the picture of Tanner's face during my visit to his condo and the stunned look it was wearing when I started linking Jim Davitsky and Ed Jones to the killings. The more I thought about it, the more I had to wonder if I had jumped too quickly into Tanner's face.

Davitsky, now, yeah—that was pretty much on the edge, too. So okay, he had a creep for a nephew but maybe he didn't know that. To use your political influence to help a relative get a job is one item. To use that relative for murder is another entirely. It takes a large jump to connect those two items. A fragment of gossip about a possible link between Davitsky and some unnamed strip joints is an item. Davitsky linked specifically to the New Frontier is another item. Again, connect them at your own risk. And keep in mind we're leaping about with a guy who takes dinner with the president from time to time.

And I had taken some damn big jumps there. The mind automatically works that way, of course. But you are supposed to audit that sort of thing, make sure it makes sense before you go around kicking doors down and getting into the face of another guy who is linked nowhere except to the creep in an official police relationship. We do not always get a choice of partners.

Granted, Tanner himself was a creep. But that was one item. Jones the creep was another. I was having trouble trying to find a bridge between the two. And all because of the look on the older creep's face when I laid it on him.

Something was not ringing together there.

So I went back to Tanner's place.

It was shortly past three o'clock. Roughly forty minutes had elapsed since my earlier visit. Time enough for the guy to get himself together in reaction to that visit. But his door was still lying on the floor inside the apartment. The lights were on. Tanner was still in his underwear. And he had a hole in his head big enough to put your hand into. The old security cop was lying curled in a corner, ditto.

I went on through, looking for the cute kid.

Did not find her, which was a relief. But I did find propped up on the dresser in the bedroom a glossy eight-by-ten nude photo of her in an erotic pose. It was inscribed in a flowing scrawl: "To Gil Honey—In Case You Forget What It Looks Like." It was signed "Tawney."

I folded the photo and put it in my pocket, poked around for a few minutes more but found nothing of interest; got the hell out of there.

I swung past the townhouses, saw the same light in the window, then went on straight to Covina and the hotel and maybe the key to this whole hairy case.

Don't mind telling you that I was coming just a bit unglued at this point. I even began wondering if maybe *I* were the key. I mean, look at it. Juanita comes to me and gets killed moments later. I rush over to her house an hour later and find her roommate freshly dead. Then I hit her place of employment and the bartender is killed. I hook up with Linda and there are two attempts on her life. So I go rattle Tanner, and now Tanner was dead. I had to figure the old night watchman as an incidental death, but he was still dead and I had touched him.

So, hell, I was counting five corpses and a sixth near-miss. In—what?—twelve hours or so?

* * *

I hit the hotel at about three-thirty and left the car up-front beneath the portico, went through the lobby and across the courtyard. Two women were sitting beside the pool in quiet conversation and sipping canned Cokes. There was no other sign of life, pretty much what you should expect at that hour of the night, but I felt creepy. Those courtyards are lighted but not enough to be intrusive. I found myself jumping at shadows.

I stood there for a minute outside the room with my hand on the doorknob just going for vibes. Didn't get any but still felt creepy. There was no show of light through the window but of course the drapes were closed. I rapped lightly on the door, then tried the key. Opened right up for me. I knew right there that the suite was empty. If she'd been in there, the safety latch would have been in place. It was not, so she was not.

I went in anyway and closed the door before I hit the lights. Everything looked pretty much as I'd last seen it. Except for the note. It was wedged into the refrigerator door.

Joe—thanks for everything but I just can't take this. I'm going out of town for a few days. You're fired.

—Belinda

*Be*linda, mind you.

Fired?

Five people were dead!

Fired, my ass.

I went back to the lobby and showed my key to the night clerk. Some of these newer hotels have the jazzy telephone equipment that keeps a record of your calls and even prints the numbers called onto your bill.

I crossed my fingers for luck and told the guy that I'd made an important call earlier but now I'd lost the number and needed to call it again. He said no problem and I said gee thanks and he pushes a button and gives me the whole printout of calls from my room.

Seven of them. Three to the same number. All within the first thirty minutes we'd been registered there.

I looked closely at the timing and decided that "Mom" must really have been worried if it took three calls to reassure her. Put the list in my pocket and returned to the suite; dialed Mom.

I got a sleepy male voice: "Yes?"

I said, "Mom?"

It said, "Who is this?"

I said, "Sorry, wrong number," and hung up.

Then I went along the list of other numbers. Got three airlines and Airport Express.

None of the airlines would cooperate in a confirmation of space for Linda Shelton when I could not tell them where Linda was spacing to.

Airport Express was a bit more helpful. I found a sympathetic ear. Told the dispatcher that my wife had run away and I did not know what name she was using but I knew she'd left the hotel in one of their vans.

He picked it up right quick; said yes, they'd made a pickup at my hotel at twelve forty-five that morning and took the fare to American Airlines at LAX for the three A.M. flight to Honolulu.

I thanked that sympathetic ear very much, hung up, chewed it for a couple of minutes, decided to call Mom again.

She still had a male voice and it was even more irritable in the pickup.

I said, "It's me. Did she get off to Honolulu okay?"

Mom sleepily replied, "Guess so. She called from the airport, said she was clear."

I asked, "Are you going over?"

Mom wondered, "Think I should?"

I replied, "It's up to you. But things are heating up."

Mom sighed and told me, "I have some very important meetings scheduled for tomorrow. Well... maybe I can work around that. Really think I should go?"

I said, "It's up to you. Me, I'd go."

Mom asked, "You getting a cold? You sound hoarse." Mom laughed in advance of the joke. "Maybe you should go for me. Aloha would do you good."

I did not laugh. I said, "That wouldn't help you much, would it. Speaking of that—"

Mom came right back with: "I know, I know. Don't worry about it. You'll be properly taken care of. Just don't let this thing spill over."

I said, "Well, it is already spilling like crazy."

"I know, I know. But let's contain it all we can. Tell you what. I'll go to Honolulu. I'll book a flight for tomorrow afternoon. I'll be back on Monday. And I want to come back to a well-contained situation. Think you can handle that?"

"I'll handle it."

The guy chuckled, said, "Take care of that cold," and hung up.

I put down the phone and stared at it for a long moment.

I had never spoken to the man before; would not know him if I was sitting across the table from him; but I had the most certain feeling that "Mom" was Jim Davitsky.

Which was okay.

But my heart was squeezing for Linda. Okay, it was squeezing on my own behalf, too. We do not always enjoy the truths we find, as I had learned a long time ago.

CHAPTER FOURTEEN

I HAVE A FRIEND on the Honolulu Police Department. Met him at a cop convention years ago in San Francisco and we had some laughs together. Have a lot in common. His name is Billy Inyoko. Japanese. Billy and I have kept in touch over the years but we have not spent a lot of time together. We are telephone friends. We exchange favors. I was a bit short on the exchange because the islands get a lot of our bad asses while theirs tend to stay closer to home.

So I was not at all reluctant to call Billy at that hour of the morning, only a couple of hours past midnight on Oahu. I caught him at home with one foot in bed and told him about Linda. Well, not everything about Linda, but I gave him an inch-by-inch description and her flight number and asked him to look in on her arrival and get a line on her whereabouts when she settled in somewhere.

Billy sounded a little tired but he assured me that he would do that. We jawed for a couple of minutes about other things and then I casually mentioned Jim Davitsky. He knew the name.

"One of your esteemed politicians," he remarked.

I said, "Yeah. Know the guy?"

"By reputation, mainly. He's got a place out near Diamond Head. Comes over from time to time. Does a lot of entertaining. Mostly political. Came the last time with a group of congressmen from Washington. We get security assignments out there from time to time."

I casually inquired, "Ever get the White House bunch out there?"

"Not the main man, no, not yet."

"What does that mean?"

"It means he does get the White House bunch. In dribbles and drabbles. Yeah, we get a lot of action from your man Davitsky."

I told him, "Keep the head up. You might be getting a lot more. This woman could be headed there."

"She'll be in fine company."

"What does that mean?"

"It means a lot of women head there every time Davitsky does."

"That way, eh?"

"Oh yes indeed, very much that way."

I said, "Matter of fact, Billy, I have some inside poop

that Davitsky might be coming over your way later today. You might, uh, keep an eye on him too."

"Sorry, pal."

"What does that mean?"

"It means that the favors end where my chin begins."

"That way, eh?"

"It's a small island, Joe."

I told him, "Message received. I'll still appreciate a line on the woman, Billy."

"You'll have one."

I thanked him and we said good-bye.

I then shook down the hotel suite, looking for anything, found nothing. I made some coffee and drank it, had a fruit snack, checked out at five A.M.

Had to get moving.

I was expecting a sunrise service at my place.

And I did not want to miss any of the festivities.

I knew these guys, but barely. All three of them. Detectives. Clones, more or less, of Gil Tanner. But only one, I think, was San Gabriel Division. They were waiting for me in my driveway.

I do not live in a neighborhood, exactly. Only four homes are built along that particular ridge. Each has a two-acre lot, and each is landscaped for privacy. My neighbors have horses. I hate horses, and I especially hate the flies that keep them company. You might find this surprising but I do a lot of gardening. It's my way to relax.

Anyway, I have privacy there. I can walk all around my place bare-assed and the neighbors would never know unless they went out of their way to keep tabs on me.

But nobody keeps tabs, up there.

It's a tabless society, up there in the hills, and we like it that way.

Well . . . most of the time we like it that way.

I was not so sure about this time.

These guys were really pissed at me. Like disturbed hornets. Or an Apache war party.

I got out of my car and leaned back against the roof, lit a cigarette, said, "I'll tell you guys why I sent for you."

"Do that," growled Vince Garbanzo. We called him Beans.

They were standing in an arc, an arm's length apart at about three paces out. Flanking Garbanzo were Frank Cruz and Tony Dilivetti. None of these guys was soft like Tanner. They were bad-asses and enjoyed it. Dilivetti held a baton.

"You're going out of business," I told them.

Dilivetti scratched his head with the tip of the baton and said, "Do tell."

I said, "Well, technically, you're already out of business."

"I think it's the other way around," said Garbanzo.

"We don't need your kind in the valley. We figure it's time you're moving on."

"How far would you like me to move?" I inquired. "Six feet? Straight down? Like Tanner?"

That gave a pause. They exchanged glances. Dilivetti asked, "What's that about Tanner?"

"Someone prepared him for the move. Put a hole the size of a baseball in his skull to cinch the deal. You boys know nothing about that?"

"When was this?" Garbanzo asked.

I sighed. "Little while ago. Changes nothing, though. Except to point the way. Good-by, boys. It has not been nice knowing you. I want your asses moving and I don't want them stopping within smelling distance. You fold up your tents and you steal away, a long ways away, or else I'm—"

Dilivetti took a step forward with the baton at combat stance. Garbanzo put an arm on him, said, "Wait, Tony"; said to me, "What's your interest, Joe?"

"Call it the stars and stripes forever. I still believe in the Constitution, human rights, all that stale, corny old stuff."

Cruz uttered his first words. "Get this guy. The original hard-ass. I never saw you bleed for anybody, hotshot. Where do you get off laying that rap on us?"

I told him, "I get off where guys like you get on, Cruz. Now back off. Go back to your barrio and work your scams on the sad devils whose backs lifted you up here. Maybe one of them will decide who the real enemy is and show you the way home. I got no respect at all for an Indian who eats other Indians. Get your rotten ass off my turf, Geronimo. You're overfertilizing it."

What did it take to get these guys fighting mad?

Cruz just blinked at me.

I took a drag from my cigarette and told Garbanzo, "Let go the Dago, Beans. He wants to play."

Garbanzo did, then, and Dilivetti did.

He came at me with the baton.

I used it to lever him off the side and over the car.

He hit the hedges at the other side of the drive.

By this time, though, I was in a sandwich between Garbanzo and Cruz, and Cruz was going for my balls.

I gave him his own, instead, and hoisted him by them into Garbanzo's face.

They both tumbled down, with Cruz howling.

I stepped on his face because I cannot bear to hear a grown man cry.

Then I took a ground-level charge from Garbanzo and diverted it into the side of the Cad.

He hit like a Ram in the rutting season; went down; stayed down.

But now I had Dilivetti again.

His face was like oozing hamburger from the thorny hedges but the eyes were pure crazy.

This time he came with gun in hand but in his rage had neglected to thumb the safety. I beat him to it and crunched the arm apart with the back of the elbow across my chest.

He screamed and fell to both knees. A bone was protruding from the sleeve of his jacket.

Cruz was still squirming around the ground, moaning.

I picked him up and tossed him into their car, did the same for Garbanzo.

Dilivetti stopped groaning long enough to tell me it had all been a mistake.

I agreed with that and suggested that he get in the car and drive the mistake elsewhere.

He was bloody and hurting, but somehow he managed to do that.

I watched the carload of mistakes lurch out of my drive, and I felt good and I felt bad.

Good because all of us cousins to the apes take a certain satisfaction in a good fight well-fought.

Bad because I knew that those guys were not the answer to my real problems of the moment.

And because I knew that my real fight had only just begun.

CHAPTER FIFTEEN

I STUDIED THE MESS in my bedroom for several minutes before I started cleaning it up.

The whole thing with Linda Shelton was out of focus.

If I was buying Davitsky as my villain and Ed Jones his henchman, for whatever reason, and if by some hook or crook Linda was in their camp, then her place in the puzzle was fuzzy as hell.

Why the attempts on her life? Or were they?

Why the frame with the gun in the death of George the bartender? Or was it?

Could Jones have gone after Linda without realizing that he was subjecting her to friendly fire? Possibly, sure; but, if so, then how loose was this thing?

The shotgun attack on my bedroom seemed for real

enough. But as I was standing there in the debris and studying the angles, nothing was for sure. The fire had actually come nowhere near the spa.

Let's say, okay; the first round was purely in the dark because he was working with one-way glass. After that first round, though—and there must have been eight to ten more—he was like standing at a shooting gallery at the county fair, firing at point-blank range with nothing to distract or interfere. Why was all that fire so ineffective? Intentionally so?

The little duel with the cars on the mountainside seemed in retrospect just as half-hearted.

So what the hell was it all about?

Or could it be—could it possibly be?—that Linda was striding through this whole thing a total innocent? Did it make her guilty of anything at all, the mere fact that she was on friendly relations with a powerful politician?

And if so, had she—and this worried the hell out of me—had she then jumped from the frying pan into the fire by turning to Davitsky for aid and comfort at an especially troubled time? He was powerful, no question. Women, including smart women like Linda, were known to go for that.

I was going crazy inside my head.

I did not *know* that Jim Davitsky was dirty. I did not *know* that Ed Jones was anything but a hot dog looking for some relish.

I did not *know* a goddamned thing.

Which was what was driving me crazy.

So I turned to a problem I could do something about. I cleaned up my bedroom. Then I brought in some leftover paneling I'd been storing in the garage and used it to patch the shattered window.

I was feeling a little better after that. So I went to the kitchen and built some breakfast, ate it quickly, then went to the living room to sit in an easy chair with a riot gun across my lap to catch a few winks.

I slept for two hours like that.

Then I showered and shaved and put on some fresh clothing that did not smell like death, and went downtown.

I got to the county offices at precisely nine o'clock and found Edna Sorenson at nine-oh-one.

We went into a little conference room. She brought coffee to keep me busy while she rounded up the necessary people. These were all ladies, three of them plus Edna, and we had a nice informal gossipy conversation.

I assured one and all right up front that I intended to use in any way possible any and all scraps of information I could take away from there; I also pledged on Edna's friendship that I would protect my sources into the grave.

I heard some interesting things.

Put any of those ladies on a witness stand and they could not have told you much. Most of it was hearsay, rumor, gossip. But I was not interested in the technicalities and I was not trying to build evidence. I was trying to work toward an understanding of the situation I was in; trying to dispel the crazies.

I did gain quite a bit in the way of understanding. But I did not dispel any crazies.

I was out of there at nine-thirty and streaking toward the San Gabriel foothills; as good, that is, as you can streak on a Thursday morning downtown. But I was on the Foothills Freeway before ten o'clock and I reached the New Frontier about fifteen minutes after ten.

The joint was just open. There were no patrons.

One bartender and two girls were on duty.

There was no music and nobody was dancing or even naked.

The girls looked like hell hung over.

One of them, I know, had been working the night before because she did a double take on me as I entered and went quickly toward the offices at the back side. I went over to the bar and sat down.

A big guy came out of the office, looked me over, went back inside.

The other girl approached me cautiously; timidly inquired, "Can I get you something?"

"Have any coffee?"

"Sure. Just a sec."

"Pure black," I called after her.

She brought the coffee in a styrofoam cup and put it in my hands.

"Send that guy over here," I said in a quiet voice.

"What guy?" she asked nervously.

"The guy in the office."

She went away without a word.

I watched her into the office. The bartender smiled at me and I smiled back. He turned away and went to work on his backbar setup. There was no remaining evidence of the mess I'd made in there the night before.

The manager came out and sat down beside me. I guess he was a manager. Head bouncer, maybe, bookkeeper—who would know, these days? He lit a cigarette, offered me one. I accepted it, didn't like it, lit one of my own.

Meanwhile he was telling me, "I understand you're the one who tore the place up last night."

I dropped my lighter into my pocket. "Yeah."

"For God's sake why?"

I shrugged. Pulled out an oldie. "It seemed the thing to do at the time."

He smiled. "Mighty Joe Copp."

I smiled back. "I was provoked. At least now you know my name."

"My apologies. I'll try to see it doesn't happen again."

I produced the picture I'd taken from Gil Tanner's bedroom and handed it to him. "I need to talk to this kid," I said amiably.

He studied the photo for a moment, said, "What makes you think you'll find her here?"

"I guessed. I'll need her name and address, please."

He handed the photo back and gave me a sour look. "You know we can't give out that information."

"I agree that ordinarily you should not. But this is not ordinary. It's about life and death, to coin a phrase. So I really must insist you give it to me."

"Look, Joe—"

"You look. You work underage kids in this joint. How do you keep your license?"

"You've been misinformed. All of our girls must produce two items of personal identification to get on here. We are very careful about the age business."

"Not careful enough. Juanita Valdez would be twenty next week."

He said, "Wait right here," and returned to his office.

I had time for only a sip at the coffee and a drag at the cigarette before he was back again. He placed a manila folder on the bar in front of me. "See for yourself."

It was the personnel file on Juanita. Had her picture in there, bare-ass; had also a Xerox of her driver's license and birth certificate. Both of those indicated that she would be twenty-three next week. Funny thing, though. It was the same driver's license I'd used to call her twenty next week. You can do all sorts of tricks with a copying machine. Especially if all you are going for is a phony proof of age, just for the record in case you should ever need it.

I closed the file and handed it back. "Sorry, guess I had bum info."

He smiled, slid another folder my way. "Would you like to verify Tawney Matthews too?"

I smiled back, opened the folder, made a mental note of the home address, handed it back. "Thanks. That's all I needed."

"No provocation this time?"

"See?" I said. "Could have been this easy last night."

"It gets a little crazy in here some nights."

"Crazy enough for Jim Davitsky?"

His smiled faded. "Who?"

"Guy that owns the joint. Didn't you know that?"

"You're wrong about that. A management corporation owns this place. Three more just like it."

I said, "Okay," and went out of there.

But I had not been wrong.

Jim Davitsky owned the management corporation. And Jim Davitsky was a pervert. I got that from an unimpeachable source. I can't identify that source because I promised on Edna's friendship that I would not. But the lady is in a position to know, and she knows a lot.

She'd even attended a couple of his parties; one of them in Hawaii. With all the president's men.

CHAPTER SIXTEEN

IT TURNS OUT THAT Tawney is really Sandra Matthews and lives with her parents in a very nice home in San Dimas. Both parents work so Sandra is home alone; she recognizes me through the peephole in the door and is instantly terrified, but I quickly learn that it is not so much me that terrifies her as the mere fact that I am there.

I hear her gasp, "Oh my God," through the peephole.

So I tell her, "Simmer down, Tawney. We need to talk. Open the door."

"Please go away. I'll talk to you at the police station."

She thinks I'm a public cop.

"It's better we talk here," I insist. "But not like this. The whole neighborhood will hear us."

I can almost hear the agonizing on the other side of

that door. Common sense prevails, though; I hear the bolt slide open and the door opens about six inches. She speaks to me through that slit, in a very shaky voice. "I guess you found Gil."

"What was left of him, yeah," I say. "Let me in, Tawney."

She opens the door all the way and steps away from it.

The kid looks terrible. She has been crying a lot; probably has not been to bed. She is holding a little pistol; looks like a toy but I know that it is the real thing. I hold out my hand. She drops the pistol into it; stands there looking like she is about to start crying again.

I put an arm around her and walk her to the kitchen.

"Make some coffee," I suggest.

She woodenly goes about that small chore while I am talking to her. "I am not with the police. Used to be, but not now." I put one of my business cards on the drainboard in front of her. "I won't pretend that Gil Tanner was a friend. But I have known him a long time. I went to his place last night to give him a message. He was alive when I left there."

She gives me a quick and curious look. "Yes, I know that."

"Who came after I left?"

"A man from building security, I guess. I heard them talking. I was in the bedroom. Getting dressed. Then another man came. Gil was yelling at him. Then I heard the gunshots. I hid in the closet."

"You didn't see the killer?"

She shakes her head, puts the coffeepot on the stove, turns to give me a level gaze. "Didn't have to see him," she tells me. "I recognized his voice. It was Gil's new partner, Ed Jones."

I use both hands to sit her down at the table; I take a chair across from her. "You're sure of that ID?"

She gives me the level gaze again. "I am absolutely sure."

"So why didn't you go to the cops?"

She replies simply, "He'll kill me, too, when he finds out I was there?"

"Not if he's behind bars."

"He's a cop," she says. "They don't arrest cops."

"Sure they do. Sure as hell they arrest cops who kill other cops."

She shakes her head vehemently. "Gil was afraid of Ed Jones. I mean really afraid. He told me that Ed Jones has friends upstairs, very powerful friends. He warned me never to cross him, said he's a psycho and worse than that he's a psycho with a license."

I stare at her for a moment, then ask her, "License for what."

"Whatever he wants, I guess. I don't know exactly what he meant by that. But I do know that Gil was really afraid of him."

"So why didn't he get himself another partner?"

"He wanted to. But I think he was afraid to even try."

"Why do you think that?"

She shakes her head and mutters something I do not catch.

"What?"

"I just know that Gil wanted away from that guy."

"But he felt that he couldn't do that?"

She stares at me for a moment. "He knew he couldn't do that."

"How close were you with Gil? In love with him?"

She gives a sad smile. "He was old enough to be my dad. But he could be very nice. Before Ed Jones came along I thought Gil was God. But we just sort of... not love, no, not like that. We sort of comforted each other, I guess you might say."

"How old are you, Tawney?"

She gives the sad smile again. "Around here, please, I'm Sandra. I'm twenty-three."

"For real?"

She nods her head. "For real. My parents don't know about Tawney. I'd rather they didn't."

I tell her, "No way to prevent that now, is there."

She looks down, picks at the tablecloth. "I could just leave town."

"Forget it. I'll go with you to the cops, if you'd like."

She shakes her head. "They'd just twist it around. I was there, so I must have done it, or know who did. No thanks."

"Do you understand that Gil was not the first to die?

Juanita got it; Juanita's roommate got it, and George got it. Did you know that?"

She murmurs, "I didn't know about Maria."

"Did Gil talk about the others?"

"Not much. But I know that he was very upset."

"Did he tell you who did it?"

She shakes her head, raises frightened eyes to mine. "I just know that he was scared, really scared."

"And so are you."

She lets her breath go in a shuddering sigh. "I am scared silly."

"Do you know Jim Davitsky?"

"Who?"

"The county supervisor, Davitsky. Ever meet the guy?"

She says, "Now... wait a minute."

"Okay, I'm waiting."

"I think that's the guy... Juanita knew him. Or—no, wait!—it was Maria, Juanita's roommate. Maria is pretty wild—I mean, you know, like anything goes—but Juanita was telling us one night..."

"Telling you what?"

She surges out of her chair and takes the coffeepot off the stove; grabs two cups; pours the coffee.

"... it was me and—let's see—and George... and Linda. Linda is the house mother. We call her that. She's the senior girl. Juanita was—"

"Linda Shelton. Bewitching Belinda."

"Yes. Juanita was all worried about Maria, this mess

she was in with this guy, this big shot. I'm *sure* that's the name, Davitsky, that's the guy."

"How long ago was this?"

"Oh, just a few weeks ago. Davitsky... yes, that's the one."

"What kind of mess?"

"I don't remember... just... some kind of trouble. I didn't hear all of it. I just kind of walked in on it. Juanita was having a talk with George and Linda. It was in the dressing room. I walked in and they were talking about this."

"But you don't remember...?"

"Had something to do with the talent pool, I guess."

"What talent pool?"

"You know."

"I don't know. What talent pool?"

She sips her coffee; gives me a trapped look. "We're not like hookers, you know—I mean... life would be a lot easier if we were, and we'd make a lot more money. But we work for our money, and we work damned hard for it. It looks easy, sure, from the other side. Try it from our side, for just one week, try it."

"Damn it, Sandra, what talent pool?"

"There's this pool of sexy girls, see. Not hookers, not professionals that way, but girls who know how to get a bunch of guys all excited. So Linda and George decided, I guess, that here is a handy pool of talented girls that can be counted on to be a lot more fun than a bunch of flat-on-their-back hookers."

"George *and* Linda decided this."

"Yes. They started talking up this idea about six or seven months ago and they signed up a bunch of the girls."

"Signed up for what?"

"For the talent pool. Well, okay, you know what kind of talent I'm talking about. But this was big time. Not sleazy guys in sleazy motels but big shots and fancy places. And groups. Always groups."

"Parties."

"Right. And everything done with class. No money changes hands. I mean, not on the job. Our money comes directly from George and Linda."

"Good money?"

"Better than a sixty-forty split with the New Frontier. And a lot more fun. Some of these jobs are like a vacation. You know, a weekend on a yacht or at some swank resort."

"Or in Hawaii."

She gives me a wondering eye. "Why are you asking me if you already know?"

"I know nothing, kid. You're sure this was all George and Linda's brainstorm?"

"I just know they started talking it up. At first there wasn't any pressure on the girls to join up. Guess there still isn't, except as new girls come to work at the club. Pretty fast turnover, you know. I told you it's hard work. So the girls come and go. Some stay forever, of course. I've been there four years."

"But you're only twenty-three," I point out.

"Big deal. You can get it at fourteen if you're built right. Now, especially, if you think right."

"What do you mean?"

"Well, now you don't make the tryouts unless you first sign up with George or Linda."

I am not enjoying this conversation.

I ask Tawney/Sandra, "Did you sign up?"

She drops the gaze. "I've had a few weekends here and there."

"Any in Hawaii?"

She shakes the head. "All local."

"Any involving Jim Davitsky?"

"No. I just heard the name, that's all."

"Ever hear Gil drop that name?"

She gives me another curious look. "Not that I remember."

"But Juanita was complaining—"

"Her roommate was having some kind of trouble with this guy."

"Was Maria part of this talent pool operation?"

"I guess so."

"But she never worked at New Frontier."

"No."

"Did Tanner know about your talent pool?"

"Of course he knew. He was part of it."

"Part of it," I echo.

"Security part."

"Security for who?"

"For everybody. All of it. Nobody could get busted or get in trouble with Gil's men on the job."

"How many men did Gil have?"

"Quite a few."

"All of them cops."

"I don't think all of them were real cops."

"Okay. Anything else you'd like to tell me?"

She smiles wanly. "Yes. I'd love to tell you it's all a bad dream. I'm going to wake up in a little while and I'm still eighteen and just now starting to plan my life."

"It's not too late to do that, kid."

"I feel so dirty."

"It washes off."

"It will kill my dad."

"He might surprise you. Would you like to go with me, now, to talk to the sheriff?"

She shakes her head. "I'll have to think about that. Are you going to turn me in?"

"No. But I'll feel terrible, kid, if you end up dead like the others."

"He is a psycho, isn't he."

"Worse than that, I'm afraid."

"How can you get worse than that?"

"Tanner gave you the answer to that," I remind her.

"A licensed psycho," she remembers with a shiver.

"Afraid so."

"What kind of world is this?"

"We made it, kid. All of us. We made it."

I don't know if she believed or understood that.

But I understood it, and I believed it.

One of the old Greeks, one of those early philosophers, said that a people have the government they deserve.

He was talking, I guess, about tyrants and that sort of thing—and he was talking about the country they deserve, too. Well, we're a government of and by the people.

And we've made this sucker what it is, you and I. We did it to ourselves, pal. And we've got nobody but ourselves to blame for afflictions like the Jim Davitskys.

I felt like I had an answer for the Davitskys among us.

What was giving me trouble, at the moment, was the bewitching Belinda. I had no answers whatever for that one. But I damned sure meant to find some.

CHAPTER SEVENTEEN

IT WOULD BE A SEVERE UNDERSTATEMENT for me to say that I was disappointed in the way this case was turning. The only one of the principals I really cared about and wanted to bring through smelling like a rose was instead smelling more and more period with every new development.

I refer, of course, to the bewitching Belinda.

I really did not care, now, to learn any more about the lady.

And I damned near walked away from the whole thing, right there outside Sandra's house. I did not, after all, have a client, and it was now obvious that I was not going to have a client in this case. This case? What case? I had no case. What I had it seemed, was a passel of whores and their pimps, and somebody was knocking them off. Whoopee. Meanwhile I was out two hundred bucks in expenses.

But I couldn't let it go.

I'm too selfish. Just couldn't stand to think of some strutting savage getting away with this kind of stuff. I mean, I live here too, you know. It's the only damned place I've got. Give it back to the savages, where am I going to sleep tonight? In a cave?

Besides, I had not given up entirely on Linda.

Whatever, I could not walk away from it.

So instead I went back to Ed Jones's townhouse. It was a few minutes past noon when I got there. Half a dozen preschoolers were playing in the street. A little boy of about three was riding a stick-horse. He pulled a toy gun on me and I raised my hands but the little shit shot me anyway.

I said to myself bullshit, I'm not falling down for you, kid; you shot me with my hands in the air, what kind of game is this?

I went on up to Jones's front door and was confronted with the same game played on a different stage. Ed wasn't home but his expectant wife was, and evidently he'd beaten her since the last time I was there. She had a black eye and a split lip, bruises on the throat, bruises on the arms; dress torn half off of her; I would not have been surprised to find footprints on her swollen belly.

The door was ajar and I could hear her crying from

the porch so I went on in. She lay curled on the couch; gave me a startled look as I went through looking for Jones. I didn't find him, needless to say, and I guess it's a good thing because I would have killed the sumbitch with my bare hands if I'd found him there.

I stopped off in the bathroom and wet a towel, found some disinfectant, carried it back to the couch and went to work on her hurts. She'd stopped crying; seemed very embarrassed by the whole thing. Why are battered wives always embarrassed for their pricks? I'll never understand it; and here's one for you judges: it ought to be justifiable homicide to catch the sumbitch in his sleep and blow him away. I would never collar a woman for a crime like that. I would look the other way and smile all the way home.

Well, I was smiling this time, too, but it could not have been a very good smile. She kept assuring me that she was okay but I went on with my business and cleaned her up, checked her belly, insisted she get up and show me she could walk without staggering.

Her name, by the way, was Inga, and Inga was a hell of a woman. Something else I don't understand is why these great women so often seem to end up with the class pricks. I'll never understand it. Guess I don't want to understand it. I am fighting like hell becoming a total cynic but I think I've almost lost that fight.

Anyway, that's the way I was feeling there with Inga. She told me that Ed came home around six o'clock.

His left hand was bandaged and his clothes were torn and dirty. He was driving a car she'd never seen before. He refused breakfast, took a shower and shaved, would not answer any questions, lay down with the alarm clock and slept until ten o'clock; got up, got dressed and left before ten-thirty.

She gave him my message as he was leaving. He came back in and beat her up when she had the nerve to ask what was going on with him.

I told Inga I was going to bust the guy. I told her the whole rotten story as I knew it. She did not seem surprised at any of it.

And she did not try to beg me off.

Instead she told me, "I wish to go home for my baby."

So I told her, "Today would be a great time for it."

"I have been thinking of it," she replied.

So I said, "Pack a bag." I snared the telephone. "You want Lufthansa?"

She showed me a smile. "I have no money."

I said, "Who needs money?"—and called information for the number.

Twenty minutes later we were on our way to LAX. She was traveling light; most of what she put in the bag were things she'd made for the baby. She owned only one other maternity outfit beside the one her husband had torn off of her, and she was wearing it. She showed me her smile as she was packing that bag and told me, "I came without. I go home the same way."

I put her on the three o'clock flight and told her, "You're not going home without, kid. You've got guts and dignity."

She said, "Thank you, Joe," and gave me a warm kiss good-by.

I was out another seven hundred bucks, thanks to my groaning Visa card. But what the hell. I was going to nail that lady's husband—that unborn baby's father. Not that I was trying to buy off my conscience. I have no conscience where people like Ed Jones are concerned.

But I was just as happy to have the lady and the baby out of the line of fire that I was sure was coming.

While I was at LAX I decided to shop around for flights to Hawaii. I went on down to American for the first try and made my score there. Told the guy at the ticket counter that I had some papers for Supervisor Davitsky but couldn't remember the flight number. He obligingly punched it up and gave me a four-thirty flight to Honolulu.

It was already past three so I went up to the gate area and killed forty minutes over a very expensive dinner at the cafeteria. Could have dined at Chasen's for that tab. But the food was okay and I was starving and it was a good way to wait out the clock.

I wanted to eyeball the guy.

After dinner I bought a copy of *Penthouse* and a large manila envelope from the newstand, put the magazine in the envelope and wrote Davitsky's name on it, took it to the check-in counter and asked the agent to please be sure that the supervisor received this important package before he boarded the plane.

The guy said sure thing and made a note on the seating chart.

I found a seat in the lounge with an unobstructed view and settled into the wait with a cigarette.

I had the guy spotted even before he picked up the envelope.

I mean, you know, he just looked big deal. About six feet tall, sort of rangy—maybe a hundred and seventy pounds—fortyish, clothed by Gucci, I guessed, certainly the shoes were Italian leather: not a bad looking guy if you were not looking for bad, which I was.

Two guys came in with him. One went to the check-in for the boarding pass while the other bent an ear to a stream of words. The one returned with the envelope and two boarding passes, turned the whole thing over to the Gucci. There was some discussion obviously centering on the envelope. Davitsky finally opened it, took out the *Penthouse,* laughed and looked around as though to see who was playing the gag on him; returned the magazine to the envelope and slid it under his arm.

The three stood there in their little circle talking without a break in the flow until the flight was on final call. I was playing a little game with myself over which one of the other guys would board with Davitsky.

As it turned out, the game was on me.

Ed Jones sauntered into that circle as the final call was going down. Davitsky handed him a ticket envelope and a boarding pass, shook hands with the other two, then he and Jones strolled to the boarding gate.

There I sat with my hardware stashed in my car.

Jones was no doubt wearing his. A public badge will get you through the weapons check. A private one will not, which is why I was not wearing mine.

Uppermost in my mind, of course, was the idea that "Mom" must know for damn sure by now that someone had played a telephone game in the middle of the night; but still he was going on to Honolulu.

So I what-the-helled it and hurried over to the check-in and gave the guy a stock urgency pitch. He took me to the gate and passed me on to the boss stewardess, a pretty woman with a patient smile who no doubt had handled many last-minute no-ticket passengers. She took my Visa card and sent me on inside. It was a DC-10. I caught a glimpse of Davitsky and Jones seating themselves in the First Class cabin. I went the other way, of course, toward the tail, where I planned to remain until we reached the Fiftieth state.

Don't ask what I was doing there.

I did not know myself, at the time.

It just seemed that my "case" was moving to Hawaii. And I could see no point whatever to my remaining behind.

So, what the hell.

Aloha.

CHAPTER EIGHTEEN

A DC-10 IS ONE BIG AIRPLANE. When you think about it, you wonder how the damned thing gets off the ground. Guess I never really understood the principles of flight—and I also guess, when you get right down to it, that I don't want to understand. Some things are better just taken on faith. For me, airplanes and flying fit that category. Probably wouldn't bother me at all if I was sitting up there flying the sucker myself; assuming, of course, that I knew how. I don't like to feel helpless in any situation. Like even in a car. I want to be the guy with the hand on the wheel and the foot on the accelerator. On a packed freeway, of course, hurtling along within a tight clump of speeding vehicles, that in-charge feeling is probably ninety-nine percent sheer illusion. But at least there is comfort in the illusion. All you get on one of these big airplanes is a feeling of total dependency on other people's competence. You can't even see the guy who's flying it; hell, if you're back in the tail, he's a block away. I even have to assume that somebody *is* flying this sucker. Could be a machine up there flying this machine, so far as I knew.

As I started to say, the DC-10 is a big machine, so I had no particular worry about encountering Davitsky or Jones while we were in the air. All the seats were not filled but there were still, I figured, more than three hundred people aboard, and just about all of those were seated between me and those two. Also, the First Class cabin, as usual, was draped off from the other cabins while in flight.

I had the very last window seat and nobody was assigned to the aisle seat beside me—which was good because my body does not fit well into these tight spaces. Soon as we were airborne I pulled down the window shade, pulled a blanket up over my head and went to sleep. It had, after all, been an eventful twenty-four hours with damned little sleepytime. It was a five-hour flight, and I slept all the way.

One nice thing about jetting west is that you can pick up five hours of sleep while the clock ticks off only three. We landed at seven-thirty on the dot, Honolulu time. I was among the last to leave the plane, though. Did not want to tip my hand at this stage of things and felt pretty well assured that I knew where these guys were headed.

However, I did pick up a little bonus inside the terminal.

Davitsky and Jones were standing off to the side of the swirl of deplaning passengers, obviously waiting for something. They were not looking my way. I stepped off to the other side and lit a cigarette—which is usually the first thing I do when I come out of an airplane. It was then I spotted the bewitching Belinda. She was walking fast and looking anxious; late for the pickup, no doubt.

No doubt was right. She spotted my turkeys and went straight for them. I winced as she seemed to hug Davitsky, then watched as he introduced her to Ed Jones. Jones shook her hand and said something in deadpan. She said something back, semi-deadpan. I said to myself okay, damn it, and watched them walk away.

I was going to tag along at a distance but then I got another bonus.

My pal Billy Inyoko materialized from out of the crowd and put an arm on me. First time I'd seen him in the flesh in a long time but it could have been yesterday for all he'd changed.

Let's get it into the record, here. Billy is a fourth-generation islander and a one hundred percent American—one hundred ten percent American cop. No Mr. Moto here, understand; no inscrutable oriental. One of my suits would probably come apart and make three for him, but the size of a man has to do with a lot more than physical dimensions. This guy was very large in my respect.

He said to me in an almost chiding tone, "If you'd told me you were coming I'd have arranged a lei reception for you."

I replied, "Yeah, well, I didn't tell myself until I saw those buzzards getting on the plane together. Did you eyeball them?"

"Davitsky and friend, yes," he said. We were following along far to the rear of the passenger flow. "Who is this friend?"

I told Billy who is the friend, and I'd told him all I knew about the guy by the time we got outside. We stood in the crowd and watched while the three subjects climbed into a waiting limousine and took off. Another car rolled smoothly to the curb and a door flew open in front of us. Billy pushed me toward it.

We got in; Billy introduced me to the driver—guy named Howie, which is purely a phonetic spelling because the guy is Hawaiian and I don't know from all those vowels in the lingo—and we took off in pursuit of the limo.

I reminded my pal, "Thought this island was too small for a tangle with our politicos. So how come you're here to greet the man?"

He in turn reminded me, "I'm a cop."

"You were a cop last time I talked to you, few hours ago."

"But that was before I found an angle on all this."

"What angle?"

He showed me a tight smile. "String of unsolved murders, Joe."

"How long's the string?"

"Long enough maybe to stretch from Los Angeles to Honolulu."

"That long."

"Yeah."

I asked, "Starting when?"

"Starting nearly a year ago. There have been four deaths with similar patterns. Last one was about a month ago."

"What's the angle on Davitsky?"

He gave me an oblique smile. "He was on the island for every one."

"Yeah, that's an angle."

"Or a coincidence. But I have to check it out. Right?"

"Right."

He said, "This boy Jones... how long with Davitsky?"

"Not that long, I think. He was in Germany until six months ago."

"Your deaths on the mainland," Billy said. "All young girls?"

"Them, too, but also a gay bartender pimp and a kinky cop. It started as girls."

Billy nodded, then told me, "We seem to have a serial killer on our island, Joe. Either that or we've got one of yours who comes here for his kick."

I asked, "How high the kick?"

"High as it goes, I guess. It's the sadistic sex routine. All our girls died very hard."

"Ritualistic sadism?"

"Coroner thinks so. One of them was pretty badly decomposed and the sharks had been at her before she washed up. But on the other three he points to evidence of wrist and ankle clamps, other types of restraint devices. All of them had their sex organs practically ripped out of them."

"You've got a sick one."

"Maybe we've both got a sick one—maybe the same one. If your's is mine, Joe, you've got yourself a really terminally sick son of a bitch, let me tell you. Wait 'til you see these girls."

I told him, "I don't want to see your girls, pal. Have enough trouble sleeping as it is most nights. What do you have to tell me about Linda Shelton?"

"Nothing much. Came in like you said. Rented a car and drove out to Davitsky's place. Stayed inside the whole time until she came back for Davitsky."

"What kind of place does he have out there?"

"Big joint. Estate. Several acres."

"On the water?"

"Sure. Boat docks. Helicopter pad. Very swank."

"Service staff?"

"That's one of the oddities," Billy said thoughtfully. "Just an old couple there, like caretakers—live in a garage apartment, I take it. You'd think a multimillion dollar joint like that would rate a couple of maids, if nothing else."

I said, "Well, if you bring your own maids with you ... and you have a need for privacy ... and if you want to keep your dungeons off limits—"

"I don't want to find anything like that out there, Joe."

"Does that mean you're going looking?"

He gave me a sharp glance, settled back into his seat. "Of course I'm not. *You* are going looking."

Fancy that. It was exactly what I had in mind. But I was feeling a trace of discomfort with what Billy Inyoko might have in his.

CHAPTER NINETEEN

OUR FIFTIETH STATE has a rather unique political setup. There are only two levels of local government, state and county. Honolulu itself is both city and county, coextensive to include the entire island of Oahu. It may surprise you, as it did me, that Honolulu is now ranked as the eleventh largest U.S. city, with a population close to a million. There is no municipal government, however.

Southern California could maybe take a lesson here. Because there is only one police department for the entire island. Police-wise, there is but one level of government; there are no state police, Jack Lord and Hawaii-Five-O notwithstanding. So there are no jurisdictional lines and/or political squabbling over police responsibilities. The Honolulu department polices the whole island, and they do it quite well.

I give you that little bit of background just in case you are wondering about Billy's reach beyond Diamond Head. It's like telling an L.A. city cop to go make a collar in Santa Monica or Glendale. He can't do it, not legally, which causes a bunch of problems in an area where invisible political lines create artificial distinctions for law enforcement. But that kind of problem does not exist on Oahu.

It must have been a twenty-five- to thirty-minute run from the airport to Davitsky's home away from home. Diamond Head, in case you've never been there, is that majestic headland rising to the southeast of Waikiki Beach that you see on all the postcards. Actually it is the cratered remains of an extinct volcano that blew its head off in prehistoric times. It also marks a corner of the island. Go on around Diamond Head and you start heading slightly northerly for the first time since leaving Honolulu International. It is a very picturesque area—the Kahala coast—and quite a relief from the highrise jumble at Waikiki. There are also some fine homes in the area, of which Davitsky's was probably not the finest nor even the most impressive.

It was impressive enough, however.

A beautifully rolling lawn with flowering tropical

shrubberies and trees behind white walls provided a pleasing framework for the rambling low-profile residence. Two smaller but similar buildings nestled close by, the whole thing seemingly connected by covered walkways and further laced together by whatever they call a patio in Hawaii—lanai, maybe? Whatever, it was a nice effect as viewed through Howie's binoculars.

The limo dropped the subjects and headed back toward town, so I figured it for a hire and Billy confirmed that. Two other cars were standing outside the garages. One of them, according to my astute Honolulu colleague, was registered in the state to Davitsky and the other had been rented at the airport by Linda Shelton on her arrival earlier.

We watched the three inside. There was no evidence that anyone else was present there.

My hosts then took me on to a swank hotel nearby, not your standard digs for the budget vacation, but what the hell, I'd already shot my budget for the next two months; what did it matter. But it turns out that Billy has a friend in management there, so I got visiting-head-of-state treatment at a rate that had to be pure honorarium. Didn't even seem to matter that I checked in without luggage; Billy took care of the formalities and handed me my key.

He also handed me the keys and claimcheck to a car and a validated temporary permit to carry a gun. Which was great except I had no gun to carry. Billy told me to look in the glove box and he also asked that I conduct my visit with all possible discretion and decorum. I promised to do that, and I promised also to keep him informed of all developments.

Then he left me to my own devices.

Which shows you that my pal Billy did not know me quite as well as he thought he did.

So I thought.

I went into a convenience shop with conveniently late hours and bought an appropriately casual outfit. For me that's not easy but I lucked into some reasonable fits; took the stuff to my room and changed. Felt just like a tourist when I went down to the coffeeshop and stoked up a bit.

It was close to ten o'clock when I claimed the car. I am thinking practical joke when I see it. It is one of these Japanese sub-subcompact models and just possibly I might outweigh it.

But it is surprisingly roomy inside, once I get folded in.

The weapon in the glove box is a Smith & Wesson auto pistol, model 59. It's double-action, packs a fourteen-round clip of 9mm Luger; nice piece, clean and oily and ready to go. Fits snug and flat into the waistband of the wash-and-wear slacks I am now wearing. Two boxes of reloads are also there and a spare fourteen-round clip is loaded and ready, too.

I am wondering if all this was planned especially for me or if it is just a Billy Inyoko standard operating procedure to stash arsensals on wheels about the countryside.

But how could it have been planned especially for me if everyone was as surprised by my visit as I was?

Of course, it took me five hours to get there, once I had decided to go. A lot can happen in five hours.

So...

Was it pure chance that Billy was there to meet me at the airport? Or did the guy have eyes on L.A?

The papers on the car showed it to be the property of a local rental agency and checked out as "HPD Complimentary" at five o'clock that afternoon.

I went back inside the hotel and called Billy.

Took about ten minutes to run him down.

I asked him, "How'd you know I was coming?"

"Saw you get off the airplane, Joe."

"You knew before that, pal."

He chuckled. "Maybe I had a premonition."

I was not chuckling when I told him, "Maybe someone helped you get it."

He said, "What's your problem?"

I said, "My problem is who helped you get it."

He said, "Cops are a nasty and suspicious bunch, aren't they."

"They come by it honestly. Are you going to level with me, Billy?"

"Sure, I knew you were on the plane. How else

could I have cleared the path for you?"

"Exactly what do you expect of me here in Honolulu?"

He sighed. "At the least, Joe, we're hoping you can take care of your own garbage."

"Like that, eh."

"More or less."

"More or less what?"

"Like that."

What was I saying a while ago about your inscrutable Orientals? Suddenly I realized that I did not know this guy at all. A weekend drinking buddy in San Francisco many years ago, then a voice on the telephone from time to time, some mutual respect for efficient police work... that was it.

So what did I actually know about him?

Damned little, and most of that secondhand.

I asked my increasingly scrutable oriental pal, "How far does more or less extend? Where do I stand after a shootout, if it gets to that?"

"I guess that would depend on where you've put your feet down. You can't expect us to give you a blank check over here, Joe. Play it straight and you're okay. But you'll answer for excesses here the same as anywhere."

"But you want me to handle the garbage."

"That would be nice."

"Nice for you."

"Nice for everyone, yes. This is—"

"A small island, yeah. It's likely to get smaller, Billy, before I leave it. Want you to know that. But surely you already know that. So I need to know. Just how wide a path have you cleared for me?"

"Joe... we've stamped your investigator's license and extended the courtesies. But all that gives you is what you have in L.A. I am just saying—"

I said it for him. "Behave myself but take the garbage away."

"More or less, yes."

"You know something, Billy?" I told him, "You are an entirely scrutable Japanese cop."

Maybe. But his laughter was the old one hundred ten percent American cop as he told me good-by and hung up.

I still did not know the guy.

And I had the uncomfortable feeling that he knew me a lot better than I knew him.

CHAPTER TWENTY

I WAS AT THE KAHALA ESTATE of Jim Davitsky at twenty minutes past ten, parked just up the street and casing for an entry when the outside lights came on. Two men emerged and went quickly to one of the cars in the driveway. I had to read that as Davitsky and Jones, but I was too far away for a positive ID.

Then I had to make a quick decision. Should I tail those two or should I seize the opportunity for a private visit with Linda Shelton? Tails won the mental toss as their car hit the street squealing; I gave them a block, then sent my little funny car in pursuit.

We angled northward and caught the freeway toward downtown. At that time of night it was only a twelve- to fifteen-minute run.

This was my first visit to the island since I was a kid,

so I was definitely on unfamiliar territory and crowded closer for comfort as the going became thicker.

We left the freeway near Chinatown. You don't have to know this island to know what Chinatown in Honolulu means. Its reputation extends beyond its physical boundaries. Not exactly Sin City, but close. Hotel Street features a lineup of porn shops and strip joints —where, I am told, anything goes—and that seemed to be our destination.

I lay back there and gave them room to find a place to leave their car. Then I just idled along in the barely moving traffic close enough to keep an eyeball on and watch their progress.

They went into one of the sleazier-looking joints in the first block of North Hotel. I went on by and found a place for my car, returned on foot and hit the doorway about three minutes behind my buddies from the mainland.

This was definitely no place for the genteel tourist. It was shades of old Hong Kong, in old Hong Kong's raunchier moments.

The tobacco smoke hung in there like third-stage smog from Los Angeles. Canned music provided throbbing background for two nude Oriental girls onstage doing a vertical number on each other—but the real action seemed to be offstage. I had to pay a cover charge to get in and then there was barely standing room in the joint—maybe because there were almost as many girls as guys present, and the girls obviously worked there. One of them squeezed past me on her way elsewhere and managed to give me a welcoming squeeze in transit.

Enough said about Hong Kong Charlie's.

Honolulu has traditionally been—liberal?—in its official outlook on morals. They had legalized prostitution well into World War II and clamped it down then only because of federal pressures. The world's oldest profession flourishes on the island today, I am told, and the official attitude seems to wink at it unless the display becomes too flagrant. I am talking now Waikiki and the tourist milieu. But Chinatown downtown apparently knows no restraints that amount to anything.

I was propositioned four times before I could get a drink.

With all that, I had spotted Davitsky and Jones within the first few seconds after I got inside. They'd had no problem at all finding a place to sit; were being treated like honored guests at a big booth on the side; had their heads together with two other guys, both Orientals.

I had to read a planned meeting into that, and I'd positioned myself at a stand-up bar where I could keep an eye on them. Became obvious within a short while that one of the Orientals occupied a position of authority over the establishment, or just authority period. He was getting a lot of kowtowing from the help. Now, the islands have their own homegrown version of so-called organized crime. It is probably strongest in the ethnic neighborhoods; I've heard that there's an especially strong syndicate that controls most of the action downtown. So maybe this guy was one of the local godfathers. Or maybe he was just a small-time businessman trying to get by in a hostile world.

Whatever, there was no apparent lack of interested conversation between this guy and Davitsky. I could not hear it, of course, but I could tell that the general tone was very serious.

Jones seemed to be totally relaxed and enjoying himself. A pretty Chinese girl wearing a shorty silk wrap over nothing else had slid in beside him and was keeping him entertained while the other guys talked.

I was having a tough enough time fending off the girls at the bar. I will just say about that: never has the old bod been so touched in so many ways in so short a time. It was a good thing that the meeting was a short one, because I was developing a short fuse. These women were determined and practiced. I am a normal man.

I was damned glad to see my turkeys standing up to take their leave, so glad that I didn't even mind when I noticed that they were being escorted to a rear exit.

I went on out the usual way and headed along the street amid the late-night throngs for an eyeball on their car.

My boys emerged from an alleyway, each with a girl on the arm. All six piled into the car as I pulled a hasty retreat toward mine.

I got lucky.

They eased on along Hotel street and passed me just as I was tucking myself into my own car. I pulled out six cars behind them and had no problem with the tail while we fought clear of Chinatown.

But then as we were approaching the freeway I became aware of the caravan. A third car was in that lineup—I was sure of it—and maybe even a fourth behind that one.

So I turned away two blocks from the freeway and came back in at the rear of that procession just as it hit the ramp heading east.

But I still had one behind me, and it had been there all the way from Chinatown.

Was this developing into a laugher?

I mean, if Billy had a guy on me and also a guy on Davitsky...

But of course there was nothing to say that Billy had a guy on either of us.

And if he did not, then this was anything but a laugher.

I had to know.

At least I figured I knew where my turkeys were headed.

So I turned off at a Waikiki exit and ran toward the beach.

The same dark sedan jumped off and ran with me.

Let me tell you something about the Honolulu cops.

These guys do not drive official cars. They buy their

own vehicles with high-performance engines and cruise around unmarked. There is no such thing as an off-duty cop in Honolulu. He's always armed, always ready; and he does not screw around with you. There is a law on the books over there informally called the cop-harassment law. Does not have to do with cops harassing the citizenry. Has to do with the citizenry harassing the cops.

If one pulls you over for running a stop sign and you give him any lip at all, that is harassment; and it will land you in jail, booked and fingerprinted. It also could land you a baton against the side of the head if you do not respond quickly enough.

So I did not know what the hell.

I am cruising along Kapiolani Boulevard at twenty mph in my funny car.

This black sedan with two guys up front are cruising along a hundred yards off my rear bumper.

I turn down Date—headed, I think, in the general direction of the Kaimuki district just north of Diamond Head.

Soon as I do that, this black sedan surges forward and is coming around me like fifty mph.

I get a glimpse of an Oriental face in my sideview and something that could be a gun barrel sliding up into view over the door on the passenger side.

I hit my brakes and slam toward the curb.

The black sedan hurtles past and three quick gunshots roar out of it. A plate-glass window to a shop just off the nose of my funny car shatters and rains all over me.

Two more shots come back as the black sedan plunges on. These hit an empty car parked at the curb behind me.

I am understandably upset by all this.

So I lean into the steering and acceleration at the same time and jump it back onto the street.

I have that silly little four-cylinder engine winding up like a siren and I am gradually closing the distance on those s.o.b.'s.

The S&W 59 comes out of the waistband of my slacks and I thumb off the safety.

Paradise of the Pacific notwithstanding, those sonsabitches don't get away with crap like that.

Copp for Hire is in fast pursuit in his funny car. And he does not much care who or what he finds up there in that black sedan.

And, yeah, Paradise is definitely getting lost.

CHAPTER TWENTY-ONE

MIDNIGHT COULD VERY WELL BE a peak hour around Waikiki. I had not been around long enough to do any studies on that but I knew that some of the bars—those with dancing facilities—were allowed to stay open until four A.M. For sure I knew that the town was definitely perking at midnight with many vehicles on the streets and a lot of foot traffic.

So this was not the best of all possible times for a running gun battle along the city streets.

Actually I did not have that in mind.

I just wanted to climb onto that rear bumper and hang there like glue until my shooting buddies either stopped to confront me eye to eye or found a nice quiet street where we could play out the string in relative solitude.

Apparently they did not want to do either.

The guy was shooting at me through his own shattered rear window, at damned near point blank, and my funny car had shaken off three hits when I decided I needed to revise my options. Either I had to break off and let them go, or I had to return the fire. But then something intervened in my decision-making process. I don't know if the guy was trying a funky maneuver to get me off his rear bumper or to line up a better shot for his triggerman—or maybe he was just paying more attention to me in his rearview than to his own driving—but suddenly the big car braked and swerved toward the center of the damp street. He overreacted; the sedan spun out, did three pirouettes along the dampened street, clipped a parked delivery truck, stood on its nose for a moment, then slammed on for a couple of end-overs before coming to rest on its roof in the center of an intersection.

I went on through and parked on the other side. People were running to the scene from everywhere and several cars had stopped nearby. I am still not sure of the exact location, but Diamond Head was straight ahead a very short distance and a golf course bordered the intersection on two sides.

I saw no evidence of cops, so I pushed through the spectators and began shouting warnings about the possibility of fire and explosion, which sent most of them toward an uneasy withdrawal. But a small group of diehards remained clustered about the wreckage trying to help the occupants.

I could have told them they were wasting their time.

Two guys were crumpled inside the wreckage. All the windowglass was gone, the top was caved in and pinching into the head area. Blood was all over the place. One of those guys in there I had seen before. I did not ID that from the face because it was upside down and distorted and covered with blood; everybody in that condition looks pretty much the same. But the clothing was fairly memorable and I'd seen it earlier in a booth at Hong Kong Charlie's. Not the Godfather or whoever but his companion. The guy with the steering column in his chest was just another stiff.

I reached in on the passenger side and tugged a wallet loose from an inside coat pocket.

One of the helpful citizens gave me a dirty look. I gave him one back and he looked away for assistance. I dropped the wallet into my pocket and walked away, joined the growing crowd and went on through it, got to my car about the time the emergency sirens were close enough to hear.

Didn't check out the wallet until I was well clear of the scene.

The guy's name was Daniel Woo.

He was thirty-eight years old, five-feet-eight, one hundred and thirty pounds.

And he was an officer of the Honolulu Police Department.

* * *

I was mulling over what Billy Inyoko had said to me about getting my feet down in the right place, and wondering how I could have possibly put them down in a place more wrong. But let's keep the perspectives clear, here. I was feeling no remorse over the fact that the dead man was carrying a badge. A kinky cop, as you've gathered, is the worst thing in my book, at the head of the list in front of psychopathic killers and rapists and you name it—because a kinky cop is a *traitor* of the worst kind, a scumbag who uses his badge to defeat and disgrace everything the badge stands for.

Enough guys like that and the badge stands for absolutely nothing... except maybe a swastika. And the less the badge means to the average citizen, the harder it is for the good cop to do his job. Brings back to mind Honolulu's harassment law I mentioned earlier. What that really says to the citizen is you've got to respect the badge. Don't argue, don't alibi, don't resist; the man is at least out here trying to do a job so behave yourself and let him do it properly and without resort to force. Imagine what it would be like if every cop had to draw his weapon to win a debate over every exercise of his police authority. The cops are overwhelmingly outnumbered, you know. Take a city like Honolulu with upwards of a million residents and maybe four to five million visitors a year. I would guess the Honolulu force at something under two thousand officers for twenty-four-hour coverage 365 days a year. How does such a handful police a town like that unless the average citizen at least respects the badge?

I guess a lot of armchair constitutional lawyers would take a dim view of that Honolulu law, which at first glimpse seems to butt against individual rights. Well, I think it's a good law and it should be universal and universally enforced. Save the lip for the courtroom; let the cop write his ticket or make his collar as efficiently and peacefully as possible and get on with the job of protecting the community.

Okay, so that's how I feel about the badge.

But I did not fight a badge. I fought a guy who'd already trashed his own badge, and I've no apology to make for that. Besides, the guy was dead on his own initiative; dead while trying to make me dead, for a reason nowhere connected to his badge.

I did feel, though, that I'd put my feet down in quicksand. It could suck me under at any time. And I had to wonder what the hell I was doing over here on this alien turf, anyway. I'm a private cop, for God's sake, in business for myself and very probably headed into bankruptcy. I had no client and therefore I had no case, was not even on expenses. So who the hell, you might ask, commissioned Joe Copp to police the world and save society from itself? You'd have a point.

I resumed the track and headed on out to the Kahala district. I was no more than ten or fifteen minutes behind as the result of my eventful little detour through

Waikiki. I was in a slow burn—mostly at myself—and kicking my own ass all along the road in my funny car with bullet holes.

I wondered if I should check in with Billy Inyoko, and then wondered why the hell I should.

And, I have to tell you, I wondered if I should just tuck in the tail and go on home like a sensible citizen too far out on a limb.

By this time, though, I am idling past Davitsky's place and noted that there were now three cars in the driveway. Lights were on throughout the main house and both bungalows; also I saw lights and activity down along the boat docks...

It appears that a party is getting underway. Seems like a strange time for partying, especially considering the circumstances, so I park directly uprange and watch. I hear female laughter and see figures transferring stuff onto a boat. It is a deep-sea cruiser, maybe a fifty-footer; I'd noticed it earlier during the look-see with Billy Inyoko but the dockside lights had not been on at that time and I'd seen little more than a silhouette in the twilight. Now the boat, too, is lighted inside and I can make out a good-sized salon topside...

So what the hell; I left my vehicle parked along the roadside and went over the wall for a closer look. I was able to get inside about a hundred feet without exposing myself. Probably I would have had a hard time attracting anyone's attention out there, short of shooting off a gun or going on board with them. They were having a great time loading the party provisions and making ready to cast off.

Davitsky was on the bridge and warming the engines.

Ed Jones was fiddling around with the lines, obviously an apprentice at this seamanship business but ready to do or die for good old Jim.

The Godfather or whatever, a vigorous guy of maybe fifty, was helping the four Oriental girls stock the bar and put away the groceries.

I caught not a glimpse of the bewitching Belinda.

Davitsky gave his signal from the bridge, and Jones cast off the bowline, then ran aft to cast off the stern and scramble aboard via the swim platform. The cruiser nosed smoothly out of the slip and moved quietly into the darkness.

I lit a cigarette and stood there until the boat was out of sight, then stepped onto the walkway and went up to the house.

The bewitching Belinda met me with a pistol in my belly.

I said, "Aloha, kid."

She said, "You are one crazy man."

Hell.

She did not have to tell me that.

I'd been telling it to myself all night.

CHAPTER TWENTY-TWO

I'VE SAID I BELIEVE a person is revealed by their home but I guess I don't know what to say about the home away from home. I think maybe the home away from home could reveal our secret fantasies; as though to say, okay, while I'm here I'm somebody else. And you set up the vacation home to reveal that somebody else.

Of course I had never seen Jim Davitsky's home in L.A.

But this joint here on the island was bizarre, to put it mildly.

A party pad, obviously, and put together with that idea supreme in the planning. But it was opulent, gaudy, vulgar in a no-holds-barred stretch for sensuality, coming together as unrestrained erotica.

You got the feeling, walking through all that, that Jim Davitsky fantasized his "somebody else" as the Marquis de Sade. And you got the feeling, too, that this "somebody else" might just be unhinged—considering the context.

I mean, here is a guy with all the money anybody could ever want. True, he was born to a lot of it but he had more than tripled his net worth since he came into his own, so the guy had to have some business smarts. He was young, good looking, rich, popular in political circles; guy like that could reasonably entertain national political aspirations with maybe even an eye on the White House some day. After all, look who else has made it.

So what does this guy want, you could ask, that he does not already have?

Looking around this home away from home, it seemed pretty obvious what Jim Davitsky really wanted. And that "want" was clearly out of context with his many other assets. I mean, I was trying to picture this place as the Hawaiian White House, the president's home away from home, and the focus simply would not resolve. I am talking life-size copulating statuary, art-deco Kama Sutra wallpapers, the erotic art of the masters hanging from the walls, huge oversized sectional sofas upholstered in llama fur, funny chairs designed to accommodate every possible sexplay positioning, a white marble hot tub in the living room complete with retractable serving trays and even an "oriental swing" suspended overhead—and all that is just what's up front.

Hey, I'm no prude. I enjoy a bit of erotica from time to time the same as anybody. I'll swing from a chandelier now and then, if I can find one to hold me. But to be totally immersed in it is, to me, to be immersed in some head problem. To be immersed in it to the point of self-destruction is akin to alcoholism or drug addiction.

My reading on Jim Davitsky did not all come from the Hawaiian home, of course. But taking everything together, I figured I had my line on the guy.

Linda Shelton more or less confirmed it.

She had nervously but determinedly refused to hand over the big pistol she'd met me with but made no move to stop me as I went on inside for a look around. We passed no more than eight or ten words between us and things were decidedly stiff as I showed myself around the joint, then I hit her with it straight from the hip.

"Are you really a psychologist?"

"Yes."

I deliberately eyeballed the surroundings and invited her to do the same. "Look around and tell me what you see."

She clutched the big pistol with both hands as she perched on a stool at a bar loaded with phallic symbols

—even a brass bottle opener that was actually an eight-inch dildo. "We tend to see what we want to see, Joe."

I lit a cigarette, blew the smoke at her, settled down across from her; told her, "Don't give me that clinical stuff. This guy has a problem and you've been feeding it. So why don't you put that in your doctoral thesis?"

She gave me an angry look; said, "You really enjoy the leap to judgment, don't you."

I picked up a heavy ashtray designed as a reclining nude woman; you figure out where the ashes go. "I leap at what I'm given. Give me another and I'll try it on for fit."

She slid off her stool and confronted me with both hands tightly pushing the gun towards me. "You have no right barging in like this. I asked you to butt out. Why do you insist on dogging me around? I mean, really Joe. All the way to Hawaii?"

I wanted to laugh in her face but instead turned to an inspection of the bar. "Come on, Linda, you're a bright girl; you can do better than that. No *right*? People dying all around me, people invading my home and shooting it up, couple of attempts on my own life—I've got no right? If I can't leap at this, kid, you tell me what I should be leaping at."

Her gaze dropped, the gun with it, and it seemed that her anger was losing its focus. She turned away from me. "Joe . . ."

I was not enjoying this, not even a little bit. I said,

"Just to save us both some meaningless time, I know about your little talent pool enterprise."

"I see."

"I don't. Maybe you could enlighten me. Give me something else to leap at."

She lowered herself onto one of the furry sofas, looking beautiful but also vulnerable as hell; placed the pistol on a table at her knees, delicately pushed it away from her. The outfit she was wearing was not designed for dispassionate viewing, a fluffy thingamabob over a sheer leotard that only highlighted the natural endowments thereunder. She lay back with her hair fluffed onto the furry background, sighed heavily, kept the eyes averted as she told me, "God, I'm tired, Joe. Haven't slept since... don't remember when. It's a nightmare."

I said, "Yeah. Let's compare your nightmares with mine. Start with the talent pool."

"You won't believe me. You want to believe the worst. Go ahead. Be my guest. Call me whatever you came to call me, then please get out of here before they come back."

I said, "You still don't get it, kid. I came to call you nothing. I came after some killers."

She looked at me, then; at her pistol, out of reach; back to me again. "Including me?"

"You do seem to be rather comfortably installed among them."

She raised to an elbow, regarded me soberly for a

moment through half-closed eyes. "Guilt by association, huh?"

I shrugged. "Not to mention, birds of a feather and all that. What am I supposed to think?"

She said in a dulled voice, "Obviously you think like a cop so I guess you're supposed to think what you're thinking. I really don't care, Joe. At this point, I really don't care."

"Okay, you owe me nothing and it works both ways. But satisfy my curiosity. Why are you tangled up with this guy Davitsky?"

"He's my boss."

"So I gather. But when did you find that out?"

She lay back down, began picking her words in a rather careful recitation. "Private audience one night. He called me back, told me how much he appreciated my so-called art. We talked. One thing led to another."

"Culminating in what?"

She looked around. "All this."

"Uh huh. But take it backward several steps."

She sighed. "Ever think of it?" she asked a moment later. "Most of our troubles begin very small, so small we don't recognize it as a trouble until it has grown large enough to devour us."

I suggested, "Put it in your thesis."

She replied, "Maybe I will."

"Put it to me first."

She raised both knees and crossed them, interlaced

her fingers behind her head, looked sort of dreamy for a moment, then said, "He was very charming. Nice looking. Fabulously successful. Very political, powerful. Did a lot of entertaining. Told me he was always in need of attractive women to help him entertain important visitors. Made sense. I was always worried about these girls out moonlighting on their own. Never knew what they'd run into. Jim's proposal made sense, at the time. So I talked it over with George. Look, the girls were already doing it. And in a highly dangerous way. We figured we could elevate the process a bit, do everybody a favor."

"Including yourselves."

The lady was apparently beyond anger now. "Sure. Why not? Nobody pays my bills for me. I'd been knocking myself out for years with very little gained. If I am going to perform a service I should be properly paid for it. Do you work for nothing?"

"Lately, yeah," I replied. "But not out of choice."

She sat up suddenly, clasped her knees to her chest, shivered. "I don't know why it should matter but I can't stand what you're thinking about me."

"Maybe I'm just your mirror."

She stared at me through a moment of heavy silence, then said, "There is that, too, I guess. Something of a psychologist yourself, aren't you."

"Most cops get that way."

"Some laboratory you've got, huh."

"We get it all, yeah."

"Joe... please believe... okay—I admit that this whole idea fascinated me. Jim is an exciting man with a very exciting life... including many interesting people. Someone I once studied in school, maybe Freud, said there's a little bit of whore in every woman. Maybe that's true, and maybe there's a whole lot of whore in me. I found it exciting. No, I found it positively fascinating. It really turned me on to be around such stimulating men, I mean powerful men who are shaping the future. But I—please believe this—I did *not* know the party was going to get rough."

I nodded my head at that. "Usually we don't. Or there wouldn't be a party. As for your future-shaping fascinating men, though..." I let my eyes stray about the room again, silently inviting her to do the same. "What shape, you figure, do they have in mind?"

She said, "I didn't know about this. Well... okay, I'd heard about it. But... somehow it just didn't translate this way." She looked altogether miserable; dropped her gaze to inspect her own knee. "I know what you're thinking."

I told her, "I'm thinking your boy is certifiable for the loony ward."

She nervously rubbed her knees. "Maybe so."

"So why'd you run to him?"

"You won't believe me."

"Try me."

"I'm still not sure about any of this, you know. I mean, I don't know for sure what to believe about Jim. I just know that Maria—Maria Avila, she was Juanita's roommate..."

"I know. Go on."

"Maria served notice that she was out of it. Now Maria is... well, as I think I once told you, Maria would go for anything. If enough money was involved, she'd take you in a cesspool if that was what you wanted. But even she was scared, really scared, and she flatly refused to take any more assignments for Jim Davitsky."

"The last job she did take was...?"

"Here, yes. She and two other girls came with Jim and two men from Sacramento for a weekend. I guess Maria was Jim's girl and—"

"Have you ever been Jim's girl?"

She met my eyes firmly. "I'm nobody's girl. And this is my first time in Honolulu."

I said, "Okay. Prerogatives of the madam."

She showed me a sour smile. "Remember that."

"So Maria...?"

"She came back from Honolulu very upset. Announced that she was out of it. But Jim would not leave it at that. He'd taken a special liking to her, it seemed. And then I believe Maria threatened him with something. I don't know what. But there was some question about a video and some pictures she might have taken. All of a sudden we had the security people all over us."

"Tanner's crew."

"That's right."

"You didn't know Ed Jones."

She shook her head. "I'd seen him around the past few months. Always in the background, though. I never got the idea that he belonged to Tanner, until I saw them together yesterday."

I said, "So maybe he didn't. Maybe he was Davitsky's hedge against Tanner. Could you buy that?"

She said, "I can buy it, yes. Especially now. Seems to have come into his own. Suddenly he is very much in the foreground."

I told her, "I believe he is Davitsky's triggerman."

She blinked. "Maybe that's going too far with mere speculation."

"He's the guy that shot up my bedroom while we were in the hot tub."

"You don't know that."

"And the guy who tried to run us off the mountain."

"How do you know that?"

"Don't look so surprised. You saw the guy planting the gun that killed George in your car. You saw him shadowing Juanita before she was run down. You saw him—"

She lay back down and muttered, "Oh God."

I said, "Maria's trip to the island. She came with two other girls. Did she get back home with two live girls?"

"Yes."

"Did she say anything...?"

"No. Just that she didn't want anything more to do with it."

"Have you ever heard anything to make you think that Davitsky sometimes picks up local talent? Like tonight?"

She said listlessly, "It's practically de rigueur for these Honolulu assignments. I understand that there are almost always local girls involved."

"So why all the expense of bringing yours along?"

"Our girls are the class act, the regular companions. These local girls don't even speak English, most of them, or so I understand."

"So what do they do?"

"They perform, I think."

"Perform?"

"Yes. You know. Kinky material."

I looked around that room. "Whips and chains, that kind of kinky?"

"That too, I guess," she said quietly.

"So why are *you* here?"

She told me almost defiantly, "I came to get the truth."

"And you'll likely find it, kid. In a shark's belly. No Ph.D. at the end of this research. Didn't they ask you along on the boat tonight?"

She had gone very pale. "I told Jim I wasn't feeling well..."

"But you promised to go later," I guessed.

She whispered it. "I promised nothing."

"Don't. Your talent pool has become an expendable liability to this guy. He has knocked off at least two of your girls and your general partner. So—"

"Two of my . . . ? Maria really is dead?"

I said it bluntly on purpose, for a calculated effect: "As dead as you can get with your throat shrink-wrapped inside a G-string. They tore her place apart searching for the pictures, then tore her apart when they couldn't find them without her help. So maybe there never were any pictures. So what chance did the kid have to talk her way out of it at that point? And what tender mercies do you expect to find here at the hands of the same people?" I shook my head. "Davitsky must have thought he really had a bird in hand when you turned to him last night—"

"Stop saying it like that. I did not *turn* to him. I wanted to find out what was going on over here."

I looked around again. "Well, you found it, kid. Enjoy the view. It will very probably be your last. Somehow I just can't believe you when you tell me it's your first. You look very much at home here. Same way you looked with Jim Baby when you picked him up at the airport. You said it yourself—birds of a feather, or whatever. I guess that covers the action pretty well, doesn't it?"

She said, "What's happened, Joe? You were almost sweet. And at least understanding. Now you're so cold, and brutal . . . It's like I'm talking to a steel wall. Why can't you believe me? I know you want to. Why can't you?"

Maybe I was being cold and brutal. What I felt, though, was numb . . . just pure numb. I told her, "I've been once-burned, kid. Do you expect me to smile sweetly now and swallow the whole damned thing again?"

She lowered her eyes, quietly said, "No. Go to hell, Joe. Just go to hell."

"I'd say we're already there, kid," and I went out of there.

Linda made no move to stop me—but I did not get far.

An HPD cop was at my car. I knew why he was looking at it, and I knew what he was looking for. I clasped my hands at the back of my head and told him, "There's a pistol in my waistband. You're welcome to it."

I took the spread against the roof of the car while he took the gun and cuffed me. He did not read me my rights and I made no attempt to exercise them.

Even at that, I figured, I was in far better shape than the bewitching, or bewitched, Belinda. You go figure it. I was merely under arrest for suspicion of homicide in the death of a police officer and twenty-five hundred miles from home. Linda Shelton, I suspected, was already under a sentence of death and would never see home again.

But she'd bought it for herself.

And maybe she'd bought it for me, too.

CHAPTER TWENTY-THREE

I HAD BEEN IN A HOLDING CELL for about thirty minutes when Billy Inyoko came for me. He took me to his cubbyhole office upstairs where we had coffee and talked. They had me sewed into this thing, of course—felony hit-and-run, suspicion of vehicular homicide while resisting arrest—various other minor charges: enough to make *aloha* mean forever.

I gave Billy all the details of how it went down, then told him, "It was a hit, pal, and I was the target. How was I to know one of Honolulu's finest was the guy with the trigger?"

He frowned. "That doesn't say much for Honolulu's finest, does it. Don't worry, Joe, we've known about Danny Woo for a long time. We've been letting him play and biding our time for the bigger fish."

"About the size of Hong Kong Charlie."

Sourly, Billy confirmed that. "Yeah. Guy has very strong connections, and he's into every dirty thing on the island."

"Just how high do those connections reach?"

Billy fidgeted for a moment before replying. "High enough to give fits to every honest cop in the department. This man Davitsky has become quite a powerbroker. Almost overnight."

"That so? Even here in Hawaii?"

He growled, "Yeah. Especially here, we think. Look, the politics on this island have never been a matter of holy pride. Nothing really rotten, you understand—not that I've known about—but it has always been a good-old-boy's club. Simply translated, they take care of one another. It's a small island, Joe. Never the center of anything, forever the outhouse of mainland politics and lately the playground for the powerful who are more comfortable in an outhouse than in a Washington suburb. They feel safe here. They *are* safe here. Or they were. Until..."

"Until Davitsky and Hong Kong Charlie got to be buddies."

"Well... that's what we're thinking."

"How many important men, do you figure, have become compromised by Davitsky's hospitality?"

He shrugged. "They come and go like bats in the night."

"Never with their wives," I guessed.

"Hell no, not with their wives," he replied, smiling sourly. The smile widened as he corrected himself. "Well, maybe one or two wives. Equal time for the goose, you know, sometimes."

I said, "Yeah," thinking of that Museum de Sade out there beyond Diamond Head, and the bewitching lady apparently ensconced there.

"Anyway the thing has gone totally out of hand. We believe your man Davitsky thought he was using Charlie Han—Hong Kong Charlie—and Charlie encouraged him to think that way. Meanwhile Charlie is muscling into the local political scene using his new mainland clout. We just don't know at this point how deep the connections run. One thing we know for sure..."

I lit a cigarette, said, "It runs all the way to Washington."

He sipped his coffee, making eye contact over the rim of the cup. "You said, that. I didn't."

"If you can't even *say* it, pal...okay, right, it's a small island. So say something about where I stand in all this now."

He solemnly replied, "We're leaning overboard with you, Joe. You've got to understand that my neck is right up there beside yours."

"That's small damned comfort."

He did not smile. "It's not that bad. I've convinced

the men upstairs that you are maybe the best route into this problem. The catalyst, maybe, to shake this thing off center. So..."

"So officially all is forgiven."

He stared at me for a moment, then replied, "Let's say it's temporarily suspended. No charges are being filed, pending—"

"Pending what?"

"Pending a more comprehensive look at the situation."

"I see," I said, but I saw dimly. "My license still intact?—I mean, the HPD stamp?"

He nodded solemnly. "Naturally. You're still conducting an investigation. Right?"

"Maybe not. I've sort of lost heart for this investigation. Besides, I don't know where the hell to take it."

"Take it to Charlie Han."

"Why am I beginning to feel like the sacrificial goat? Maybe I don't want to take anything to Charlie Han. Maybe only a damned fool would take it to Charlie on his own turf."

Billy smiled. "There you go."

I said, "Thanks, but I guess I don't want to play."

"You disappoint me, Joe."

"Does that mean you took me for a damned fool?"

"I took you for a dedicated cop."

"No, you took me for a damned fool. Let's play it that way. And let's say that I've decided I am not that big a fool. I don't want to play."

Billy replied without really pausing to think about it. “Then I would have to remind you that you are under island detention.”

I said, “Remind, my ass. This is the first you've mentioned it.”

He smiled. “I told you that we've suspended judgment, pending...”

“Let's suspend that suspension, then. Charge me and book me so I can make bail.”

He was still smiling. “Hard ass, aren't you. Bail won't get you off the island, Joe. If you're going to hang around, you might as well be doing something useful.”

I said, “Bullshit. I've decided to take up vacationing as a hobby. Send on the hula girls.”

He put his hands behind his head, tilted back in his chair, laughed.

I said, “Yeah, it's funny as hell, Billy.”

He composed himself. “We have a man inside Charlie's camp.”

“Hooray.”

“They've decided that Miss Shelton should not be allowed to return to the mainland. Alive, that is.”

That sort of gnawed at my numbness, but all I said was: “Then don't you think you have an obligation to rescue the lady?”

He was entirely sober again. “How would you propose we do that? Invade the home of a powerful politician, kidnap the lady, then try to justify our actions on the basis of a tip from an anonymous informer? Or should we expose our man, prematurely close down an undercover operation two years in the building and maybe end up with nothing but a false arrest suit from a very irate 'victim' who refuses to believe that she is a victim?"

I looked at my hands because I could not meet Billy's gaze. He had me, and I knew it.

"So what do you want from me, Billy?"

"I just want you to act like Joe Copp."

"Act the fool," I translated.

He grinned. "Show me an honest dedicated cop who's not a fool."

I reminded him, "I'm a private cop, now."

He reminded me, "You've always been a private cop."

Funny, I had never thought of it that way before. But maybe Billy was right.

I told him, "I'll need a thorough briefing. Everything you know or think you know about Charlie Han and his interests."

"Naturally."

"And I'll need a writing."

"What kind of writing?"

"Something official saying that I'm under contract to HPD."

Billy screwed his face into a thoughtful frown; finally decided. "I'll try but I can't guarantee that. See, that would—that would defeat our whole..."

I finally tumbled to it, then, that these guys were really scared of Hong Kong Charlie.

"See what you mean, yeah." I sighed and thought about it, chewed it thoroughly, then told my entirely scrutable friend, "Okay. What the hell, anyway? I'm damned if I do and damned if I don't. May as well be damned for something worthwhile. But here's what I want you to do. I want you to charge me and book me in the death of Daniel Woo. Make my bail. Then just stay the hell out of my way until I come out screaming."

Billy Inyoko smiled slyly and reached for his telephone.

And why not?

He'd just landed himself a damned fool. And now he was preparing to throw him overboard again with a hook through his belly in shark-filled waters.

Aloha, my ass.

CHAPTER TWENTY-FOUR

I HAD A NEW FUNNY CAR, a new gun, and a new lease on life on the hard side. It was a short-term lease. I knew that. Leases on the hard side are always short-term. Life is like that. You find a way to spend it quietly and economically, and the leases tend to be more enduring. Start spending it loudly and extravagantly, you never know where your next step will land you. Which I guess is why most people like it better when it's quiet and controlled. Most people, I think, prefer the predictable life. The things they are doing today are pretty much the same things they were doing yesterday and will be doing tomorrow.

Which is why we have cops.

Cops are sort of like a guarantee of the status quo. And cops usually lead more or less predictable lives themselves. They patrol the same beats day after day, become attuned to the predictable patterns and rhythms and react in predictable ways when those patterns become disturbed. That's mainly what police work is all about.

But crime, you see—crime is not at all that predictable. Crime is usually always a break in the pattern, or a shift in some rhythm. It is life out of control. Someone or some group decides to step outside the normal flow and start a new cycle that respects neither the status quo nor the other guy's turf. New cycles are great, of course, if they promote something better and respect other people's rights. That's progress if they do and crime if they don't.

But I was talking about leases on the hard side. Most cops don't stake out territory over there. They visit the hard side from time to time, sure, all of them do, but in the main their lives are as predictably routine as anyone's—often to the point of boredom enlivened only by their own imagination. I mean, think of it: just driving around aimlessly all day or all night, waiting for some pattern to break down, or endlessly shuffling papers at a desk and waiting for something interesting to break the monotony. Makes me think of a scene in an old war movie where these highly trained combat troops are going crazy with boredom waiting for the war to come their way, scared that it will but even more scared that it will not. That's what a cop's life is like, mostly, anyway.

But Billy Inyoko and his people at HPD were sort of caught between the two sides of the street. They could neither relax into the monotony of a routine gone sour or effectively invade the hard side because the patterns had become too jumbled. Like a general in the field under orders to pursue and engage the enemy but receiving conflicting signals from Washington about who the enemy is, where his jurisdiction is and how hard can he fight.

That was where Billy was, and I understood that.

But I also understood where I was, and I did not like that. I was like one of those military covert operations designed to get the job done while the politicians debated what the job should be; let's all hope they will rubber-stamp the action—but if they do not... well, sorry, Joe, but of course we can't acknowledge you if the thing goes sour.

So sure, I was a soldier without a flag. Billy had given me directions to the front and a clap on the back but no handshake. Go get 'em, Tiger, sure—but don't tell anybody who sent you.

Which is what I meant by a short-term lease.

It was no lease at all, actually.

It was only a travel permit to the hard side, with no guarantee of a safe-conduct return. If there was a lease involved, then it was to a burial plot in no-man's-land, without even a marker over the grave.

I knew that. Sure. I knew it. So color me stupid.

Because I was going for it.

* * *

It was nearing two o'clock when I returned to Charlie's joint on Hotel Street. Nothing had changed except the faces on the customers—a few obvious tourists but mostly young soldiers and sailors—the same pall of smoke and the jangling canned music and pretty Oriental girls everywhere. I found room at a stand-up bar and attracted about the same kind of attention I'd found earlier, the same indelicate groping and body-rubs undoubtedly designed to incline the male mind and so forth toward the rooms upstairs. There was constant traffic up and down that stairway; I staked out a particular kid in navy whites and timed his reverse along that stairway. They were quick bangs; I timed this kid at shortly under five minutes. The girl he'd descended with was on her way up with another guy within a couple of minutes. Figure the mathematics of that, if you'd like, at fifty bucks a pop. Staggers the mind, almost, when you realize there are about fifty girls working that floor and all very busily.

I had to wonder how many joints like this Charlie had going for him, just trying to dimension the thing in my own head—and knowing, too, that the house got most of the take from the girls.

I turned away maybe ten invitational gropes before one came along who could handle rudimentary English. This one said her name was Li and seemed a bit older than most—pushing thirty, maybe. She was from Saigon, she said, and had always been in love with American men and their big baloney-sticks. She proved that by bending over and placing a delicate kiss on my slacks, and then guided my hand beneath her shorty wrap. So I fed my curiosity and allowed her to lead me up the stairway.

There was a long hallway at the top, going off in both directions, with small cell-like rooms opening to either side.

A nasty looking guy at a desk up there took my fifty, examined it and waved us on without even looking directly at me.

The only privacy in those "rooms" was provided by a beaded curtain at the door. Mine was even shredded a bit, so actually there was no privacy whatever unless there is some comfort to be found in semi-darkness. One small lamp with about a ten-watt bulb provided the only lighting. I have seen closets larger than that room, and the "bed" was nothing more than a thin pad on the floor, several inches shorter and not much wider than I am.

I have to say that Li was very pretty, but she'd lost her spontaneity the moment my fifty hit that desk. Now she seemed tired and resigned to another tussle on the pad. Or maybe she was just glad for the quiet break. She was shucking her wrap as she moved through the beads at the door, draped it on the back of the only piece of furniture in there—a canebottom chair—and set a little hourglass-type timer beside the pad. "You want suck or fuck?" she asked me in a dulled voice.

I said, "Relax."

"No time relax," she informed me. "Five minute limit." She turned over the hourglass—or the five-minute glass, I presumed. "You want suck or fuck?"

I asked her, "What became of all that adoration for American men?"

She gave me a noncomprehending look and sank to the pad, moved onto her back, raised the knees and spread them, clasping them in her hands. "You want give suck?"

I chuckled an sat on the chair.

She dropped the knees, rolled over, peered at me across a shiny shoulder, tiredly said, "You say."

"I said relax," I reminded her.

She replied, "Okay. Relax. Look." Then she began moving into various acrobatic positions.

I put a hand over there and stopped that. "You *relax*."

The kid was just trying to please. She rolled onto her back and lay still, eyes closed, but reminded me, "Five-minute limit."

She had the business phrases down pat but very little else to command English, I decided, but I told her anyway, "I come talk Charlie."

She opened one eye and found me with it. "Fifty dollar talk Charlie?"

I showed her a grin. "Yeah. Dumb, huh. I come

work Charlie. Charlie good work?"

She closed the eye, waited a beat, then replied, "Go away."

I said, "Need work Charlie."

"Charlie no work American men," she quietly advised me. "Charlie work China men, Viet men, China girl, Viet girl. American men dumb, huh. No work Charlie."

We were doing okay with the lingo, after all.

But the lingo was not the problem.

The problem was the guy at the doorway.

He was a big Asian; he was a bad-ass and he looked very upset. He said something angry to Li in her own tongue. She scrambled off the pad and grabbed her wrap, ran out naked.

I bent down and turned the hourglass over, looked up at the guy from that level and said to him, "Come work Charlie."

He put the muzzle of a Colt .45 against my throat, helped himself to my gun and said to me, "Cut the bullshit, guy. We've been watching you all night."

Fancy that. My fondest hope had just been realized.

I said, "Then you know why I have to talk to Charlie."

He said, "No, I don't know about that. But I know why Charlie needs to talk to you."

So okay, I could buy it to that point.

Okay, sure, I had to buy it. I'd already put my fifty down. On the hard side.

CHAPTER TWENTY-FIVE

IT TURNS OUT TO BE A LONG WAIT for my little talk with Charlie Han. I am seated on an uncomfortable chair in this dirty and cramped little office at the rear of the club, and time moves slowly. I do not even have room enough to straighten my legs and stretch out a bit. My back is to the wall and my knees are butted against the front of a steel desk that looks like maybe it was bombed at Pearl Harbor. It has an undisturbed layer of dust that took a long time to accumulate so I have the idea that very little business is conducted in this office; I am starting to wonder how much thicker the dust layer will get before Charlie shows up.

This jerk won't let me smoke.

He wants to know what's the matter with me, I want to endanger other people's health with my nasty habit.

I point out to him that five minutes inside that clubroom is equal to a lifetime of the paltry smoke from my cigarettes, but he doesn't buy the argument; I still can't smoke.

So I sit there fuming inside over this growingly intolerant age of ours.

He knows I'm fuming; gives me a sly grin; I get the idea that this guy is a reformed smoker and he is enjoying my discomfort. It is a familiar feeling; I get it often and I have lately begun to resent the hell out of it.

So I remind the guy about the fucking whales.

He says, "What about the fucking whales?"

I say, "Well, that's just one of the issues that mean more than this anti-smoking hysteria. How about unwed mothers?"

He says, "Yeah, how 'bout them."

I say, "Well there's an issue more important than smoke."

He reminds me that they should not smoke, too. Old people with emphysema should not be exposed to cigarette smoke, he tells me. I look around the office and don't see any old people or pregnant women, and I give audible note to that observation.

He says yeah, but what if one should come in while I'm sitting there smoking.

I say, *"Okay,* I'll put it out."

"Damage is already done, though," he says with a

shrug. "You've already loaded the air with that shit. They say secondhand smoke is more dangerous."

I decide I have this guy's game, now. He's as bored as I am. He's playing with my head to pass the time.

So I go ahead and light up anyway.

He raises his Colt and aims at a point midway between my eyes. I smile and put out the cigarette as I say, "Bullshit, how could it be more dangerous?"

"They proved it."

"Who the hell proved it?"

"Those guys in the government, that doctor, one with the beard, that general guy, the doctor general."

I say, "Doesn't make sense, though, does it? If secondhand is more dangerous, shouldn't nonsmokers be at higher risk?"

He says, "That's what I'm telling you. We are at higher risk."

I say, "Then wouldn't it be smart if we all took up smoking?"

He frowns, scratches his head. "No, see... if everybody stops smoking, then none of us are at risk."

I say, "No more cancer or heart disease?"

He says, "That's right. Well... not as much."

I say, "Bullshit. What're we supposed to die of, then? They're rigging the figures, pal. First they use the figures to say you're at risk if you smoke. Then they conveniently forget those figures to tell you that you're at greater risk than the smoker if you don't smoke but he does in your presence. That's a covert operation, pal, and they're fucking with your head to convert non-smokers into zealous anti-smokers."

"Why would they do that?"

"To give holy cause to their annoyance. To give it to you. So you can sit there like you're doing right now and watch me squirm without feeling guilty about it."

He says, "Bullshit, I don't feel guilty."

I say, "'Course you don't. You've got God on your side now."

See, this is a dumb conversation. I know it at the time. But it's the sort of thing you sometimes find yourself going through when death is looking at you. So much of life, I've discovered, is really inane. And sometimes it gets the silliest when life and death are, as they say, in the balance. Here is one man holding a gun on another man in the backroom of a whorehouse owned by a third man who probably kills and maims without qualm, and they are discussing the pros and cons of the surgeon general's warnings about cigarette smoke.

It's a parallel, see, to the larger world, sort of anyway, and I can't help thinking about that, even considering my circumstances. What were the real problems facing mankind? Weren't they hunger and poverty, crime and warfare, ignorance, injustice, slavery, misery and suffering of every kind—in wholesale lots? So why were so many Americans so fired up over so many inane goddamned issues? I am sitting here in a whorehouse with maybe fifty female slaves under roof and God knows how many pimps and killers and goons of every stripe—and we are arguing, for God's sake, the effect of secondhand cigarette smoke.

So I tell my captor, "You're an asshole."

He shrugs and tells me, "So are you, and you're a dead one if you think you're going to blow your fucking smoke at me."

I shrug back. "Dead is dead. We all get it. Right? You feel immortal? Think you'll live forever, with or without the fucking smoke? What d'you want to die of?"

"I want to die in bed. While I'm asleep. I just don't wake up."

I say, "Maybe I could arrange that for you."

He says, "Don't try. I always sleep with one eye open."

I say, "You want to die of internal causes."

"I really don't want to die at all," he says, "but when my time comes, yeah, I want to die internal."

"But not of cigarette smoke."

"That's right."

"How 'bout AIDS?"

His eyes jerk. "Not funny, guy."

I tell him, "Not meant to be funny. But if you had your choice of AIDS or smoke, which one?"

He says, "Wise guy."

"Cancer?"

"Shut up, asshole."

"You've got to choose something," I tell him. "Our

doctor generals have fixed it so there aren't many choices. You get your choice between cancer or heart attack, maybe stroke, if you want it internal. The difference between smoke or not smoke is a difference of a few years, maybe, but we all get it one way or another. So which one do you want? Heart attack?"

"I told you I'm not ready for any of that."

"Old, then—you want to die old."

"Yeah."

"Used up and worn out. Old isn't just a pile of birthdays, you know. Old is broken down. It's slow, withering—death by inches. Nothing works right anymore. The eyes go; the ears go, everything—"

"Shut up."

"Fuck you, you started it. Dying old is dying broken and helpless. You can't exercise your way out of that, pal; you can't medicate your way out of it or eat your way out of it; you're going to decay and die by inches if something else doesn't shortcut the process."

He has the Colt up again, threatening me with it. "I'm going to shortcut your process, asshole."

"So why the hell can't I light a cigarette?"

He smiles, wiggles the gun. "Because it's dangerous to my health."

"What you are doing right now, pal, is even more dangerous to your health. I just might decide any minute now to ram that damned thing up your nose and pull the trigger with your tongue."

I light my cigarette again, blow the smoke at him, put my hands behind my head.

He is grinning at me.

I blow more smoke and grin back.

"You're okay," he tells me.

"Thanks," I tell him back. "You too." I am lying. This hood is not "okay" by any standard. But it is a lying game, here on the hard side, and you have to respect the rules if you mean to survive it.

I have decided that I will survive this one.

And that is where I am when Charlie Han comes to get me.

The guy who'd been baby-sitting me was called Peter "the Saint" Fu, a native-born American and apparently one of the cadre honchos under Charlie Han. Obviously he'd gotten word on its way to Charlie even before he collared me, because he made no calls from that office. But a guy came in after we'd been cooling it there for more than an hour; just poked his head in and said, "Let's go," and the three of us went out the back way.

In passing, I noted that the club was closed and emptied, all its lights up bright and several guys cleaning up. It looked like Death City in there, under the lights, and smelled even worse.

A big dark sedan awaited us just outside. Fu pushed

me into the front beside the driver and slid in beside me; the other guy used the rear door and settled in with another man already present but nearly invisible in the shadows back there. I made contact with commanding eyes in the rearview mirror and spoke to them: "Hi, Charlie. I'm Joe Copp."

The guy seated back there with him said, "Shut up," but with no particular emotion.

Saint Peter slipped a cassette tape into a little slit in the dashboard and slapped me playfully on the knee as he settled back beside me.

The tape ran for only a minute or two but I knew what it was at the opening sound. This was Saigon Li and me during our intimate moments. They'd put us into a room wired for sound—or maybe all of them were wired.

All listened without reaction of any kind, but when it was finished, Charlie's eyes flashed at me in the rearview and he said in a flat voice, "Come work Charlie, eh?"

I said, "Well, there was a bit of a language problem there. Before I forget it, though, you owe me fifty bucks—I didn't get my five minutes."

Charlie snapped his fingers. Saint Peter reached into a breast pocket, produced a fifty, handed it to me without a sound. I transferred it to my breast pocket without acknowledgement, said to Charlie, "I figured any overture would put me in touch. But I hand it to you—I didn't expect to be in touch this quick."

He said, in that curiously emotionless voice. "You have had a big night."

I said, "Bigger than I needed, right. That's my own fault and I apologize. I didn't know that you and Davitsky are connected. I was on him, not you. Don't blame you for covering your flanks. But now I'm into deep trouble with the Honolulu cops."

All this time I'm talking to the mirror. But Charlie was reading me loud and clear.

He asked, "So what do you want from me?"

"An understanding."

"That's all?"

"That's all."

He snapped his fingers again and the car began moving. We circled around onto Hotel and went on toward the freeway, just cruising slowly.

"I do not get you, Mr. Copp," Charlie was saying, still with no emotion in the voice. "You come over here to this beautiful island and lay all over me, spy on me, knock off two of my *kanakas* and—"

"Hold it right there. I did not knock off anybody. Two boys tried to hit me but they weren't good enough so it went sour. All I did was cover myself. They got excited and got careless and got dead. I had nothing to do with it."

Saint Peter evidently felt an obligation to speak up for me. He spoke across his shoulder to say, "That's right, Charlie. I saw the whole thing with my own eyes. They loused it. Then he got behind them and was chasing them. But he didn't fire any shots. They lost it on their own."

"And one of them was carrying a badge. So that puts me in an unhappy spot."

"He tried to split," Saint Peter explained. "He did split. Went on out to the Kahala. HPD caught up with him out there. I got a read on the booking. It's suspicion of vehicular manslaughter and leaving the scene. I read it myself. He made bail, came straight to the club."

"Sounds like," Charlie commented, "you have found a brother, Mr. Copp."

I presumed he was referring to Saint Peter. "We have a lot in common." and almost choked on the words.

Saint Peter nodded. "That's right."

"You feel good about this man, do you?" Charlie asked Saint Peter.

Fu replied, "I think he's okay, sure. 'Course I don't know what—"

"Then let me tell you what," Charlie said. "This man has been a hardnosed cop for fifteen years. Could not handle the system so went out looking for trouble on his own. Thought he would bring some to our island. Now he is in a mess and yelling for help. That about it, Mr. Copp?"

I sent an angry look into the mirror. "That covers it pretty well, yeah. Except for the conclusion. I don't want any help from you, Charlie. I'm just trying to simplify my case, keep it sized right. You're not part of it."

We were moving up the hill toward the National Memorial Cemetery, called "The Punchbowl." I did not like the symbolism of that, but I tried to keep the tension out of my voice as I went on with my pitch. I was prepared to lie like hell, and thinking fast.

"I'll lay it out straight for you. Buy it or don't buy it, that's your problem, not mine; but HPD wants me to make you part of it. They've offered me a deal. Play their game and I go home clean. Otherwise, I may never see home again. So—"

"So you decided you should play their game."

"I decided I'd better make them think I am, for the moment. I don't know why they're so hot for your body, pal, but they're sure lusting after you."

Charlie merely grunted.

I went on, "I want no part of island troubles. I want Davitsky, and that's a personal want, has nothing to do with you or any of your dealings with him. Whether I get him or not, he'll take a fall because the L.A. cops are getting ready to lay all over him. I give this to you out of the kindness of my heart, and as an apology for busting in on you tonight. If you've got detectable connections there, you should break them quick and clean. The guy is going to fall."

Charlie snapped his fingers.

The car stopped.

We were within view of the memorial. A lot of Vietnam and World War dead were buried up there. I had to work to suppress a shiver as we all got out of the car—all of us but Charlie. Saint Peter shook me down again, then the guy who'd come into the club to fetch us shook me down, then the driver took a turn at it. I was thinking what the hell when Peter opened the rear door and motioned me inside.

I moved in beside Charlie. The other guys wandered away.

"I figured it was something like this," Charlie said.

I said, "Well, it does figure, doesn't it. This guy Davitsky has got a head problem."

He said sourly, "Yes." It was the closest to an emotion he'd shown yet.

I said, "You never know what comes up when you mix business with a head like that."

He said, "This man has great connections, though."

"It's those connections that are wrapped around his neck right now," I said. "And I guess that's what has HPD all excited. They're really worried about you, Charlie."

He showed me a small smile. "Yes?"

"Oh yes. I gather it hasn't always been that way. They used to look the other way. Right? Now they're looking at you with telescopes and microscopes. They're feeling heat, somewhere. But I think the heat is coming from Davitsky, or reflected off of him. Whatever, it's shining on you now and these guys are running scared—these HPD guys, I mean."

"This man has a head problem," he said. "You are right about that."

"And now it has become your problem, Charlie."

"At the moment you seem to be my problem, Mr. Copp. I do not fear this other man. Why should I fear his problem?" He snapped his fingers. "I do this and he is a dead man."

"You could do it to me."

He agreed.

"But you didn't. Why not?"

"I did not *yet,*" he corrected me, then smiled and corrected himself: "This time."

"Okay. So why not yet the second time?"

"You interest me, Mr. Copp. Particularly your story interests me, but you interest me also. Why would a man with a cop's hard nose behave so foolishly? Why do you place yourself directly into the palm of my hand . . . so close to the snapping fingers?"

"I figure it's my only way to Davitsky. He can go home any time. I can't."

"I see."

"The guy has become a liability to you, Charlie."

"We shall see."

He rolled down the window and signaled the others to return to the car.

I was watching the snap-fingers. But that hand seemed entirely relaxed now.

Mine were not. Believe me, pal, none of me was relaxed.

CHAPTER TWENTY-SIX

I DON'T WANT YOU to take me a hundred-percent literally when I tell you that Charlie Han—in a certain, curious way—is a gentleman. A hood, sure—thug, pimp, killer—all that—but with all that, something else; and the something else is what I refer to under the title of gentleman. I don't know how to sum it up except as a sort of elegance or self-possession, an almost courtly formality or dignity or whatever.

I would put him at about fifty—though I could probably be ten years wrong either way on that. He must stand about five-ten. The body is thickset, hard, probably not much fat but very substantial; he could weigh two hundred. The hands are not manicured but they are tidy and very strong, fingers thick and stubby but smooth, and the knuckles gleam when he makes a fist.

The face is not so expressive as impressive, but it does reflect the mind behind it. You get a stolid feeling there; a strength and a mindset of utter pragmatism. There is no facial hair, but it is thick upon the head, shiny black, neatly trimmed. The eyes have seen it all but still can leap with some otherwise unexpressed emotion, and they are the only place he laughs.

When Charlie speaks, you hear a hundred tongues. It is a soft voice, but soft with its own confidence and not given to postures or deceits, not trying to impress with sincerity or anger. You hear some British in that voice and some Hawaiian pidgin and God knows how many other ethnic influences, but you never get the feeling that it is groping for words or straining for effect.

In short, I was impressed with this man, while still aware that he was as deadly and ruthless as anyone I had ever met. I could have liked this Charlie Han if I had not known about the other. And I had the feeling that "the other" was what had survived many hard streets and vicious environments where only the shrewd and the ruthless make it through.

We cruised the streets and roads of Oahu shoulder to shoulder in utter silence and for quite a long time while Charlie thought his thoughts. It was my understanding that he was mentally processing the situation with Davitsky, considering his options, weighing ramifications—and I understood also that my own fate, like they say, was in the balance there. I had the feeling that he liked me, but I doubted that would have any influence on the outcome of those deliberations.

But I'd made my pitch and I knew that anything further volunteered from me would only hurt my case; I had to wait for the man to come to me for further arguments... and it was a damned difficult wait.

When finally he did speak, I was totally unprepared for it—I had let go, and maybe that is what turned the trick for me. I found myself simply going with the flow and allowing it to happen in total spontaneity.

"This man came to me as a prince of the mainland."

"Okay, sure, you could put it that way. He and four others administer a principality that stretches across four thousand square miles, eight million people, personal property valued at two hundred fifty billion dollars, with maybe the most dynamic economy in the nation. It's bigger and wealthier than most of our states. A prince of the mainland? Okay."

"Including this one, this bigger and wealthier."

"I'd say, yeah."

"This man comes to me one year ago. He brings me a business deal. I will do him certain favors; he will do me certain favors. This is the way of business. I am a man of business, not a man of politics. What do I know of politics?"

"What do you know of Jim Davitsky?"

"I know that he is a man of power."

"I presume you checked him out before committing yourself to anything."

"Of course. He is what he says he is. What do you say he is?"

"Never met the guy. But he's a prince, yeah. And maybe a devil."

Han stirred, scratched his knee, regarded me through slitted eyes. "This man tells me now that you are employed by his enemies to interfere in his business. What do you say?"

"I say I'm over here on a Visa card that's about to blow up in my face. I have no employers and I have no idea who his enemies are, except himself. I had a client, sure, for about two minutes, but she was hardly an enemy of any prince. A scared kid, that's all, with this prince laying all over her, and she came to me for help. I didn't help in time. He snuffed her. That was two days ago. Several other people have been snuffed since then, all in my shadow. I don't like it. And I don't like this prince of yours."

Eyes gleamed at me as he commented, "This is a matter of honor with you."

"Maybe you could call it that. It sure isn't a matter of money."

"Or business?"

"Not hardly. I'm not even getting expenses."

Han withdrew into another deep contemplation and we cruised through several more minutes of silence, the other men in that vehicle respectfully still but alert and obviously ready to leap to any command.

Presently Han leaned forward and snapped his

fingers at the driver's neck. We pulled into a little park and the guys again left us in privacy, withdrawing to a distance of about twenty feet but still watchful and ready to leap.

Han lit a cigar and lowered the window, so I lit a cigarette and relaxed into my corner of the seat.

After a couple of puffs on the cigar, he said quietly, "Let me tell you about this man. He comes to me with this story of connections in high places, the power of politics, and the politics of business. You say he is a devil, but..."

I give him respectful room to complete the thought, then tell him, "That was a figure of speech."

"Yes, but he has the problem in the head. I have noted this problem. He calls it business. But I..."

Again I waited respectfully, then said, "Maybe he makes a business of his problem."

That drew a sharp look, a long and careful study of my face. Finally he says, "Maybe you are right. Let me tell you this. This house at Kahala. It is a stage."

"Stage for what?"

"For business, he says. Yet I wonder. This house has false walls everywhere. It has hidden rooms behind deceptive mirrors, concealed television cameras throughout and sound devices. This entire house is a secret television studio. This man calls it the business of politics yet I sometimes wonder if his politics are not clasped within his loins. What do you say?"

I cracked my window and sent smoke outside; told

my friend Charlie, the Godfather of Chinatown: "I say he's a dangerous son of a bitch. Let me tell you how I see this man. Never did an honest day's work in his life. Born rich, with every privilege, and getting richer day by day doing nothing. Trusts no one, because he's so rotten inside himself, and feels that he owes nothing to anyone. He could be a true prince of the land, use his position and influence to make the world a little better without hurting himself in any way, yet he uses that power to gain more power. And for what? Where does it end, Charlie? It ends where it begins, I think, and you already said it—clasped within his loins."

Han nodded his head in an understated little jerk of agreement. "Ah. We see alike. I will tell you this in humility, Mr. Copp. I do not like this man. I have never liked this man. But business... well, business is business. We do not need to lie down together to do business together. But... as you say, where is the end of it? What did I truly need of this mainland prince? Why did I admit him in? What do you say?"

I shrugged. "Business begets business, doesn't it. We buy stock and sell stock and never see the certificates. Then one day we meet the stockbroker eye to eye and instinctively hate his guts. So we find ourselves a different broker. They all sell the same stock. Right?"

I got another gleam for that. He worked at the cigar for a moment, then tossed it out the window with a tired little sigh. "So what of this *haole* woman? You have plans for her?"

"My jury's still out on her."

"This *haole* woman is not his mainland partner?"

"Did he say that?"

"He infers this. Or *wahine*, maybe."

Subtle shades, there. *Haole* simply means mainlander or Caucasian. *Wahine* is the Hawaiian word for girl or woman; in this context, something more intimate than business partner was being suggested.

I asked, "Had you seen her before tonight?"

I don't know if he evaded the question or if he was simply focused elsewhere, because he came back with: "These I do not understand. For a lowborn woman, youth and beauty are her tools for survival. There are no lowborn *haoles*. So why do these highborn women engage in this work?"

"You mean whoring?"

"Whoring, yes. I do not like the word. If my *wahines* are whores then I am a pimp. I do not like this word, either."

I asked, very gingerly. "What would you call it?"

"Surviving," he replied quietly.

"You seem to be surviving rather well."

"Ah, it is beyond mere survival for me, Mr. Copp. I *have* survived, but there are levels of survival and I still must struggle. It has not been easy, let me tell you. But I am not a pimp. I am a man of business. My *wahines* are ladies of business. It is the business of survival.

What would they do? Where would they be? Boat people, you see, these are boat people. Where would they be?"

I asked, even more gingerly, "Where would they be if you gave them a fair split of the profits?"

He gleamed at me. "Ah. I do so. It is a fair split, all things considered. They have more money in one year than could be realized from an entire lifetime elsewhere. Also I give them my protection. But these highborn *haole* women . . . ah! . . . what do they need of this?"

I was thinking of a particular *haole* when I told my friend the Godfather: "I think the word is 'equalborn,' Charlie, without highs or lows out of the womb. It's not what you're born with in our country but what you do with. Some of us just go for the brass ring, without questioning what it means, and sometimes it ends up around our necks and we never find out how it got there." Hey, I was beginning to sound like a Ph.D. candidate myself. "I think your man Prince Davitsky has attached chains to a lot of those rings and I think the guy has pulled in a lot of poor fish with them. I intend to stop that if I can. If I don't someone else will, because this guy is too rotten to survive. I think you hear my words and know what they mean. You've been down all the hard streets yourself, so I don't have to tell you what it means to find yourself connected to a guy like that. He will go down. If you are connected, so will you. I rest my case. That's all I've got to say about it. You do what you have to do. As long as I'm alive I'll do the same."

He put his hand outside and snapped the fingers.

Quickly the guys were all back inside and we were moving again.

I got no conversational clues because there was no conversation.

Ten minutes later we hit Hotel Street and parked behind my rented car. Saint Peter removed the clip from my gun and stuffed it into my pocket, grinned and put the gun itself into my hand.

Beats me how these guys communicated, unless it was all set up in advance.

Charlie did not offer me his hand but he gave me a gleam and told me, "Do what you have to do, Mr. Copp."

I said, "Thanks," gave him a straight message from my own eyes and walked away clean.

Like I said, Charlie Han is an entirely pragmatic man, a survivor... and a gentleman. Well, almost one.

CHAPTER TWENTY-SEVEN

I STOPPED AT THE FIRST PAY PHONE outside Chinatown and made contact with Billy Inyoko. I found him at home, and woke him up at five A.M.

"What the hell? You've been sleeping while I'm bearding the lion?"

His voice was thick and the tongue a bit unresponsive to the demands of speech as he replied, "I figured you'd be getting some sleepytime too. Where are you, Joe?"

"Downtown. I just left Charlie. We smoked the peace pipe."

The cop was coming awake fast. "What does that mean?"

"It means there's more than one route to heaven. I

don't know, maybe you won't like the route I found, but maybe it will at least relieve some of the local pressure for a while. I believe I convinced him that he's been walking the wrong side of town. Would you guys settle for the old status quo?"

"Maybe. If it... maybe you'd better tell me exactly what you mean."

"I don't know exactly what it means. But Charlie has given me clearance to go after Davitsky. I think it means that alliance is dead. Guess you'd have to tell me what that means to the local situation."

"It could mean a lot, yeah," Billy replied guardedly. "If it's for real."

"I think it is. Look, Billy, I can't be all things to all people. I appreciate your Hawaiian hospitality and all that but I can't hum one tune and whistle another at the same time. I don't even exactly know why the hell I'm over here, but I know what brought me here and dammit I have to play my own song. I've been trying to respect—"

"Simmer down," he interrupted. "I'm not mad at you."

"Well, hooray for that. But I'm a little mad at you, pal."

He chuckled. "Hold it while I switch phones."

Funny how you can know a guy professionally for years yet know nothing whatever about his personal life. I guess I had known that Billy was married and had a family but it was a vague thing with no details attached to it. It never really occurred to me to wonder about it, I guess, but now I could see him in my mind's eye slipping out of bed and heading toward another phone so as to not disturb his sleeping wife.

When he picked up somewhere else, I asked him about it.

He said, "Sure I'm married—what do you think, I'm living in sin all these years? Hell, I'm almost a grand-pappy."

Somehow I could not picture Billy Inyoko in that role. And for some reason, trying to do that, it made me think of another guy. "Does Charlie have a family?"

"Charlie Han? Sure. I think half of Chinatown is related to him, one way or another."

It's funny, yeah. You just don't see these men that way. A man is more than his work. So why do we always judge him by his work? Oh, this guy is an accountant, that one over there is a banker, a cop or a judge or a plumber—why does that always seem to be enough to size a man?

I asked Billy, "You have a lot of boat people here?"

"Enough. Too many, maybe. Our fair share, for sure. Why'd you ask that?"

"Something Charlie said to me."

"Well, he should know. He's the big man in their community."

"I see."

"What does this have to do with anything? What're you up to?"

"You telling me you don't know? I'm not under surveillance?"

"It's a small island, Joe, but it has a lot of problems. And not nearly enough cops. I never said I was assigning you a babysitter. You told me to get off your back."

"Somehow I figured you weren't going to do that, Billy."

"Well I did. Are you saying you need some oversight now? What do you have in mind?"

"Guess I have nothing in mind. I can't go out there and put a bullet in the guy's head. I can't make a collar. So what the hell can I do?"

"What would you like to do?"

"I'd like to rattle some teeth."

"Well . . . you've got that luxury, see."

"Guess I need some info."

"What can I tell you?"

"Charlie Han, Davitsky and Jones left Chinatown at about midnight with four Oriental girls in tow. I saw them all on Davitsky's boat a short while later and they went somewhere. Where did they go? Why the party with things so tense? Did Davitsky know I was on that plane?"

"Sure, he knew. That's how I knew. We monitored a telephone call from Los Angeles minutes after your plane took off. One of Davitsky's lieutenants called from LAX and passed the word to one of Charlie's people. They had you set up coming in. That's why I put an arm on you myself."

"Great. So then you just turn me loose on a tether, staked out like raw meat inviting a hit."

"We were watching the play. Didn't I give you every support?"

"Everything but the truth. Why'd you put the collar on me?"

"Call it an interdiction. Fancy enough for you? Go on home, Joe. Hell, just go on home. I'm sorry, I—look, you're right to be mad, I had no right—go on home. I'll handle the paperwork here."

I said, "Where'd Davitsky take his boat?"

"They just went out and partied at sea. Charlie's boys were supposed to be taking care of you. They came back in at two o'clock. They were all still on the boat, all but Charlie Han, when I went to bed at four."

"The boat is back at Davitsky's joint?"

"Yeah. What are you thinking?"

"Nothing. Just sizing."

"Sizing what?"

"How the hell do I know what?"

"Go home, Joe."

"Fuck you, Billy," I said, and hung up on him.

Go home?

I didn't have a home to go to.

I knew that, see. Knew it for a long time; just never wanted to look at it. Like I said, why do we size a man by his work? Maybe that's the only size some men have. I also said earlier you can know a man by his home.

You can know me by my home, pal.

There's never anybody there but me. There's a fancy entryway and a fancy office-at-home and the fancy fucking gardens—and all of that is for nobody but me.

Go home?

I don't have a home. That was my Hawaiian illumination.

It damned near became my final one.

I hit that door with all the rage I'd been burying for a lifetime. It fell away from me, taking pieces of the wall with it, and I walked over it to get to Belinda the Bewitcher.

She knelt staring at me with terrified eyes from a llama-fur couch, and she could not run to me or away from me, nor could she call my name, because she was in chains and irons that linked the soft throat to her wrists and that to her ankles, and a sponge-ball was bound into her mouth by a silk sash. She was nude and bent into a very undignified acrobatic position that had to be painful even for a professional bewitcher.

I pulled the sash away and popped the ball from her mouth. "Sorry to invade your fun but we need a conversation."

"Jesus, Joe, get me out of this..."—or words to that effect. I'm not really sure what she was trying to say, the voice was so racked and dry and the terror so dominant.

Frankly I did not know how the hell to get her out of that. The contraption was made up of heavy galvanized steel and padlocked onto her. The guy who put her into that probably had the keys on his person, and that person was nowhere present. I had already cased the joint from the outside and found no evidence of habitation inside or out; the boat was not in the slip; one of the cars was missing; the place seemed deserted except for the trussed turkey on the llama couch.

I found some small pointed tools in a drawer at the bar, brought her some water to lubricate the throat and went to work on the padlocks.

"Relax," I told her, "it's just karma. You're paying the tab, kid, for all these years of teasing."

She was crying and laughing at the same time, whether in hysteria or simple relief mixed with pain I couldn't say, but the eyes were looking better and the words more recognizable as she said, "Promise promise promise I'll never tease again. Be careful, Joe, they're around here somewhere."

"Not now they're not," I told her, and cussed to myself as a tumbler slipped off the end of my pick without raising. Locks are not really all that complicated; you just have to push the tumblers up and keep them up while engaging the key plug, but that is easier said than done.

"Hold still, dammit," I fussed at her. "This is a delicate operation. How long ago were those guys here?"

"Seems like hours," she said, almost panting with the effort to get her emotions stabilized.

You know, I really had to give it to her; I mean, I was still mad as hell with this woman—a bit disgusted, too, I guess—but I had to respect the way she was handling herself. Some ballsy guys I've known would have been yelling bloody murder from the moment that gag came off. She was trying to work with me, and control herself—and still had presence enough to think rationally.

And she was in a hell of a fix. A heavy steel collar encircled her neck, without much clearance. The chair came down from the back of that, ran along her spinal column and through the buttocks to a double pair of cuffs. She was kneeling, with both hands drawn between the thighs and cuffed to her ankles as well as to the chain from her neck. That chain was pulled tight, no slack whatever, forcing the head into a sharp backward tilt. Very little struggling would be enough to put pressure on her windpipe and clamp off the air supply. Even to try relaxing the overextended positioning would clamp the throat. So, yeah, it was no laughing matter; I admired the way she was handling it.

But I guess I didn't want to let her know how I felt.

I got lucky with the neck lock, sprang the collar off and worked at the tortured flesh with both hands to relieve the hurt as she gratefully bent forward with the crown of her head resting on the couch. "There you go," I told her. "Next time look both ways before crossing to the hard side."

She spoke from the upside-down with a deeply wearied voice: "How many girls did I send to this, Joe?"

"Maybe not any," I told her.

"That's not true. This is what Maria found over here, isn't it."

I was working at the other lock. "I guess we'll never know what Maria found over here. She found the worst at home, that's for sure."

She shivered. "Both of them are monsters. Evil. Not very clinical of me, but they are *evil*. And I once actually thought Jim was a nice—"

"Put it in your thesis."

"Just wait until you read it."

I coaxed the other lock open and took the contraption off of her.

She sprawled forward and lay panting on the couch.

And then I heard the deep, muted throb of marine engines nearby.

Her evil men had come home.

CHAPTER TWENTY-EIGHT

I'M NO FREUDIAN PSYCHOLOGIST, as you may have noticed, but it does not take one of those to know that probably, yeah, there really is a bit of the whore in every woman—depending on your definition of whore. If, by that, you mean a woman who stands on a streetcorner and offers sex for money, then the thing doesn't wash: less than one percent of all women have tried that, I would think.

But if by whore you mean a female who uses her femininity to make the world a little nicer place for herself—then, yeah, I've seen two-year-olds who do that. Come to think of it, I've seen damned few two-year-olds who don't do that. It's genetic, part of the survival instinct threaded into sex roles, and let's hope we never civilize all of that out of our women.

For myself, I had seen no basic conflict in the idea that a bright and lively twenty-five-year-old woman struggles by day toward a Ph.D. to make life a little nicer in the long run while struggling by night with sensuality to make the same life a bit nicer, maybe more exciting too, during the short run. I didn't even see anything basically jarring in the thought that a woman could actually *enjoy* a frank display of her female sensuality in a professional sense and still be a basically good person.

I mean, hell, Victoria is dead, and long may she lay in the grave if her resurrection would signal a return to chastity belts and clitorectomies. On the other hand, I do still give lip service to the idea that sex between a man and woman should be a bit more than a casual brush in the night. Somewhere between the two extremes, though, men and women have got to come together and *find* the meaning between them; in the meantime they've simply got to come together on one basis or another, and our fractured society is making that more and more difficult every day. Hang in, this is almost over, but you've stuck with me this far, so it shouldn't hurt...

Face it, we live in an ambivalent age. We start preparing our kids in all the subtle ways for the mating frenzy before they learn how to write their own names, and the ways become less subtle as they move along. You show me a sixth-grade kid today who hasn't already mastered the subtle lessons of sensuality and I'll be looking at a culturally deprived kid.

"So the "little bit of whore" finds its natural expression via cosmetics, fashions, music, and all the entertainments. A pretty girl very quickly learns that the world is quite a bit nicer for her than for the not-so-pretty girl—that attractiveness is rewarded and the lack of it penalized—so who are we to call her a whore if she flaunts it for her reward.

I know, I know—this is sexism, some say—exploitation, some say—I say bullshit; it's the way life is and has ever been, so we may as well learn to deal with it.

I think, see, that was Bewitching Belinda's problem: she hadn't learned to deal with it. Like fire, you know, that warms our hands but also burns the flesh away if not dealt with properly; the willful exploitation of your own sexuality can do the same—and Linda, I figure, just got caught with her hands a bit too close to the flame. I think most any normal woman enjoys feeling both sexually attractive and sexually attracted. Some are bolder about it than others; that's the big difference—and maybe too some simply feel it stronger than others. But for sure every woman and every man finds comfort in the evidence of his or her own sexual attractiveness.

All of which, I realize, is an involved way of saying that Belinda danced because at some level Linda loved it, and Belinda found an easy extension into more direct sexuality because Linda did not know how to handle Belinda.

But she wasn't a bad person because of it.

I came to all this heavy enlightenment some time after I needed it, but I give it to you here, now, for what it's worth...

So while we're talking about enlightenment, including by hindsight, let's consider Charlie Han for a moment. Call him a thug, okay, but you could just as easily think of him as a minor warlord struggling for survival in a hostile world. Charlie's brutalities, I have learned, were at least confined to the requirements of his own brutal turf—and, while he is definitely a power within his own circle, it is a small circle and I can't believe that he could feel comfortable outside that circle, which means that he would have never ventured outside it if Jim Davitsky hadn't come to him with tempting overtures.

Davitsky came only because Davitsky needed a ready supply of easy femininity as grist for his mill, and because Charlie Han controlled that franchise in Honolulu.

I can't believe that HPD was really all that terribly concerned about Han even with Davitsky hovering overhead. The politics of that island state are hoary in their patterns—it is almost wholly a one-party state, and the machinations are almost totally predictable. Charlie Han already had his place in that scheme, and he'd been content with that place. He ran his own turf his own way and everybody looked the other way.

What bothered HPD, I think, was the fact of the linkage itself—between Han and Davitsky—and the possibility that Han would emerge from his "place" and look for an extension of turf. That would mean warfare in a real sense, and the surface tranquility of the island would be disturbed. The police philosophy in that troubled paradise is simply to keep the lid slightly askew while the pot gently boils. Davitsky's presence on the island together with his political ambitions was simply adding too much heat beneath the pot.

They could live with Charlie Han, if Charlie kept his place.

They could not live with Jim Davitsky.

So I guess I came to them like a gift, and they used me. I know that now. And I am not even mad about it. I would probably do the same thing, in their place.

This Kahala "resort" of Davitsky's was indeed a "stage," as Charlie Han had called it. Men like Davitsky tend to gravitate toward one another, I've learned, finding community in ways that mystify the rest of us; but they do seem to find one another, whether by chance encounter or subtle communication or whatever: there seems to be this need to get together and act out their fantasies. Whether Davitsky found his way into politics by way of this gravitation or the gravitation resulted from the politics I don't know and probably never will. But the evidence is now clear that he romped in group-sex activities with a large circle of important politicians and that he'd set his "stage" in Hawaii at great expense, a stage designed to entrap and ensnare and extend power over unwitting contributors to miles of videotape memoirs of the romps.

Apparently Maria Avila had discovered the secret video equipment. I doubt that she ever knew of any "stolen" tape; she merely invented it as a threat to keep Davitsky away from her, without realizing that the invention was her own death warrant. It also killed several people who could have been offering her aid and comfort, and it would have killed quite a few more, I'm sure, if Juanita Valdez had never entered my office.

Somewhere along his twisted trail, starting maybe even in childhood, this guy Davitsky had built one strong hatred of femaledom, and apparently it was a hatred that corrupted his sexual expression. I don't believe he was a homosexual, though there may have been tendencies. His sexual attraction was certainly female-oriented, but it was an attraction that called for domination, brutality and degradation. I give all this to you from Linda herself as a close reevaluation of her relationship with the guy, and as a result of her night of terror at his hands...

The party at sea had ended at two o'clock. Linda knows only that Charlie Han left in a huff, taking some of his girls with him. Two Oriental girls remained on the boat with Ed Jones; Davitsky came into the house and began pushing Linda around, trying to learn more about Maria Avila and what she'd known of the Kahala operation. He dragged her down to the boat and Ed Jones had a go at her. They stripped her and put her in chains and turned the Oriental girls onto her.

Apparently none of that satisfied Davitsky. The whole party returned to the house and the terror for Linda went on; she was repeatedly gang-raped by all four. She passed out at some point in the nightmare, and was alone when she came to. I showed up shortly thereafter.

That is where we are at now. It is daylight. Davitsky and Jones have returned alone from another go at the sea. I have sent Linda into quick retreat toward her bedroom. I sit at the bar facing the gaping hole where the front door had been, Billy Inyoko's pistol in my hand.

The prince and the prick stand at the shattered door, dumb with surprise. They are inside before they see me. The prince whirls about as though to run back outside, but the little prick takes a menacing step forward and goes for his gun.

"Aloha," I greet them. "Let me tell you who sent me. Maria sent me. Juanita sent me. George sent me. Tanner sent me. Finally, Charlie sent me, maybe in the name of too many anonymous China girls in the bellies of sharks."

The prince has checked himself and now stands just inside the shattered doorway. Draped around his neck are several chain contraptions similar to the one I removed from Linda.

The little prick has a gun in his hand and is frozen dumbly in a halfhearted firing stance.

They are both unsure, I guess, because I am just sitting there at the bar, and they are looking for my reinforcements.

That holds for about five seconds.

Then Davitsky says something to Jones in a stage whisper and bolts out the door; Jones flings himself toward cover behind a couch and begins unloading on me.

I just sit there, because it is not really me but an image of me in the mirrored wall. That image shatters as the glass wall disintegrates under the gunfire to reveal catwalks and video equipment.

I hear the little prick gasp in understanding but I already am on him. I rip his gun loose and hear several fingers crunch in the release. I am thinking maybe of a class lady with his baby in her belly as I decide to leave him with his head intact. I merely bang it on the floor until he quits struggling.

Then I am up and out of there, on the trail of a

mainland prince with bondage devices dangling from his neck.

I find him dancing with agitation beside a vehicle in the driveway, trying to find keys to let himself inside it.

He throws a large key ring at me and runs off toward the boat slip.

I catch the ring of keys and put them in my pocket. Damned if I know why I did that, unless it was some sort of symbolic grasping for the key to the whole mess, as though the keys were my case... and maybe the case was a key to myself.

I did not know—and still don't—what exactly Jim Davitsky represented in any big-deal larger sense. I only knew that I had to shut the guy down, even if it meant shutting myself down in the process.

It just seemed a strange place to be reenacting this ages-old drama of man versus his darker side. But then... why the hell not? It had all begun in paradise, hadn't it?

CHAPTER TWENTY-NINE

I HAD NEVER TAKEN PLEASURE or even satisfaction from any death. Guess I always believed that where there is life there is hope, and death means the end of hope. Not that I'm a Pollyanna. I have seen too much misery in this world to see it any way but the way it is. But I also have seen evil from good men and good from evil men, so I know that all our sketches are in shades of gray and the light always falls in shifting shadows that conceals as much as it reveals. So don't ask me to be God; it's hard enough to be Joe Copp. Don't ask, either, why I pursued the devil toward the boat slip; I could have turned and walked away, collected Linda, and left the whole thing to Billy Inyoko's inscrutable resolution.

Maybe I pursued because I was pursuing something

inside myself—or maybe I pursued because I knew down deep that there was no hope for a guy like Davitsky, no gray, that nothing short of death would release us from his brand of evil.

I do know that I had not thought to kill him. My gun was in my waistband and it was there as it is there for every cop, as the bottom line after all other forms of persuasion have been exhausted.

He was running for the boat, the chains swinging from his shoulders as he ran, and I was pursuing doggedly—not altogether sure what I would do when I caught him.

He halted at the dock and turned to face me, both hands up. "What do you *want*?"

I halted too, about twenty feet out, I guess because I did not know myself what I wanted.

I turned the question around. "What do you want, Mr. Supervisor?"

"I want to be left alone," he yelled. "Get out of here, get out—"

I shook my head. "No way. You've fixed it so you'll never be left alone again, Davitsky. You need a keeper. Just look at you. Look at yourself. What have you done, man? You had the world by the tail. Why'd you have to reach for the balls?"

His voice was a scream. "Don't you preach at me. Who the hell are you to be telling me what's right and wrong—?"

"Tell it to yourself. Why are you running? What are

those ridiculous things around your neck? What do they prove? Why do you need them?"

I took a step forward. He took one backward, held up the hands. "Stay back. I'll kill you. *Understand me*? I'll kill you, and I'll do it slowly. You'll suffer, damn you—"

"Why do you need my suffering, Mr. Supervisor?"

"I don't; I don't need it. *You* need it. You and all the others like you. I'll feed you your own cock, damn you."

The guy was over the edge.

I almost walked away from him at that point.

Not because I was afraid of him, or of myself. But because I knew it was hopeless, and I suddenly felt the full force of that hopelessness. What do you do with people like Davitsky? Our jails and asylums are filled with them, and it's a revolving door. I've never known of a single sex offender who was changed by incarceration or treatment. We no longer just lock the cell and throw the key away, so we mostly tolerate their presence among us.

A better way?

Short of executing them I knew of no better way.

And I, by God, was not an executioner.

So, like everyone else I was ready to turn the back and walk away.

Well...almost like everyone else.

I forgot about the victims. We all do that, don't we?

But there was a victim here who had not and probably never could forget or simply turn away.

She came running down the path behind me in a long silken robe, and she had Ed Jones's gun held tightly in both hands.

She called out, "Jim. You son of a bitch," and took up a firing stance with the gun in both hands at eye level.

I yelled, "Linda, don't," and lunged toward her.

She got off two shots before I could reach her and snatch the gun away. Both went wild, probably nowhere near the target, but they were enough to send Davitsky scrambling in retreat.

I saw him from the corner of an eye as he leaped for the swim platform of his cruiser; saw him rebound from too large a leap, teeter backward with the chains flying, then topple into the water.

By the time I got there, he was clawing toward a fingerhold on the swim platform and having a hard time finding one because the heavy metal was now tangled and wrapped about his neck and dragging him down.

I knelt down and stared him in the eye for the first time ever at close range, and I saw in there, mixed with the panic and the fear of dying, I saw God knows how many screaming, tortured girls of the past, and the devil knows how many of the future with this guy around. I saw Juanita and Maria, a shadow of Linda and maybe even of myself, dying slowly for this guy's pleasure.

"*Help me . . .*" He was flailing at the end of his chain.

"I can't do that, Mr. Supervisor," I told him.

Indeed, I could not.

I am not an executioner, no, but I am a human being, and I could not hold a hand out to that creature.

He slipped away, the eyes wide and pleading until they disappeared into the depths.

I collected Linda and led her back up the walk to meet Billy Inyoko, who, along with a goodly chunk of HPD, had just invaded the grounds.

It had not been a good case, or a neat case.

But at least it was a closed case. And I was satisfied with that.

CHAPTER THIRTY

ED JONES HAD SOME MINOR HURTS. He was transported to an emergency room enroute to jail, and Billy tells me he was screaming "deal" all the way.

Jones is nowhere in Davitsky's league, of course, but he is a natural bad-ass who probably will never get it together. I have learned that he was cashiered out of the army with some other guys for black-market activities in Europe involving stolen army goods, and there'd also been something involving brutality and profiteering against prisoners in an army guardhouse over there. Seems the army had no hard evidence on Jones for any of that; he'd dealed and plea-bargained his way clear with just a slap and a convenience of the government discharge "under less than honorable conditions."

Guess he thinks he's going to do it again, but he's into heavier stuff this time—even in Hawaii, if HPD can find some remains of the two girls he and Davitsky fed to the sharks on their final outing.

Turns out that Davitsky had been running really scared when he came over this time. Things were looking shaky in L.A. and beginning to come apart. There were also loose ends in Hawaii. A couple of Davitsky's favorites from Charlie Han's stable could speak against him, and he was suddenly worried about that. That may have been his undoing with Charlie, because I have learned that Charlie feels protective of his girls and was already genuinely uncomfortable that a few of them had "disappeared" while under Davitsky's custody.

But the guy had obviously hoped to lay several worries to rest during this visit to the islands. He had, as she'd tried to tell me, Linda on his butt; he had me on his butt; and he had Charlie Han worried and wondering. He set me up for Charlie, I feel certain, as much to compromise Charlie as to get rid of me. Surely he'd not felt it necessary to lure me onto the island if the only plan was to have me killed. He could have arranged that in L.A.; indeed, he'd already done so.

Ed Jones was the big mistake for Davitsky. I feel that in my bones. Jones is not that bright and certainly not that efficient as a triggerman. Okay enough, sure, with easy targets. Hell, a ten-year-old can put a gun to a sleeping man's head; that's no big thing. Any guy can swagger around and think tough. But not every guy can be tough and think smart. Ed Jones could not. Ed Jones is an asshole. This guy will do hard time, believe it, no matter how he pleads—and he could end up on death row if the state of California ever gets their act together. Whatever, he will find Q a bit more hostile to WASP bad-asses in the prison population than anything he ever encountered in the army, and to go in there as an ex-cop will prove nerve-racking indeed if I know my Q's. So this guy is in for no idyllic retreat at state expense, however it turns.

But he's crying for a deal in Hawaii, for sure. He has already given HPD enough to clear their slate on a string of homicides involving young women. I found a curious satisfaction in the fact that nowhere was Charlie Han implicated in those. In fact, I have heard of no charges against Charlie in any of this. I guess things are cooling back to normal and the ethnic peace of the island, as well as the political peace, is HPD's chief concern at the moment.

Davitsky was the man all the way—as far as the island killings went—though a couple of Washingtonians could get their political careers derailed through sideline involvements in a couple of those. Our friend Davitsky, prince of the mainland, was not only terribly bent, he also loved to keep photographic records of his high moments. Jones turned Billy Inyoko onto a treasure trove of such photographic moments, involving hundreds of still photos and three videotapes.

It was those photographic moments, apparently, that touched off the killings in L.A. Maria Avila had made some wild threats to keep Davitsky off her back. About that same time, a file of photographs and a short videotape came up missing. This stuff was later found in Gil Tanner's safety deposit box. Up front, though, Davitsky figured Maria as the culprit and figured that she either had the stuff or had passed it elsewhere for safekeeping. Maybe she did give the stuff to Tanner, and maybe Jones got that out of her before he killed her; whatever and however, Maria died; Juanita died; George died; Tanner died; and the list may have become endless as Davitsky scrambled to cover his bizarre indiscretions.

Meanwhile Tanner and crew had already become something of a headache for Davitsky. These cagey sleazebags knew a good thing when they smelled it and they were starting to muscle in, using the Davitsky connection as their passport and their knowledge of his activities as leverage. So all those guys had been marked for extinction, too, I'm sure. I guess I did Tanner's partners a favor by interrupting that flow. They're still alive, anyway—though they could find themselves scratching off the days in the same population with old pal Ed. You know... things could get downright interesting at San Quentin.

I hope I haven't told anything here that might sour you on the law enforcement community. A few bad cops, as they say, do not discredit the whole. And please keep in mind that in many countries of our world the police are installed by the government to oppress the people. At least in our system the cops are supposed to be our surrogates, and the badge is a symbol of our trust in one another. We're supposed to police ourselves, see. A cynical Frenchman said several centuries ago that a society can't exist unless we are the dupes of one another. I don't believe that. You're going to find corruption and thievery wherever you find human beings, sure—that's part of what we are—but the real story of a free society is that its men and women from all kinds of backgrounds at least try to work together with some respect, on the theory that that's the best way for us all.

And so I strongly believe that here, anyway, law enforcement is among the nobler professions, because its job is to service the common good, and to take care of the minority among us that wants to rock the boat.

Our cops are the equalizers against the barbarians. Please don't forget it.

And don't keep the eyes fixed on the likes of Ed Jones and Gil Tanner. Or me. I'm just a cop for hire, now. I enjoy the luxury of picking and choosing my own responses. If I don't like a case, I can walk away from it. The guy with the public badge can't do that.

He belongs to you; he wears your badge, and he always has to respond.

End of sermon. Sorry.

I am still in Hawaii and beginning to enjoy it.

Belinda does not feel so bewitching anymore, but she is starting to enjoy it too.

She is on voluntary island detention along with me for a couple more days while the paperwork flows. Same police hospitality, as a matter of fact, and in the same hotel. We had breakfast together this morning, and we have a sort-of date for a luau this evening.

She is clean with the law here in Hawaii, except as a material witness, but I am afraid she will get a slap or two when we return to California. She knows that, and accepts it. Our relationship—if you can call it that—is trying to stabilize around the new honesty. I don't know what that will bring, but I know that I will be opening all the doors I know in L.A. to keep her official record clean. She's going to be a damn good clinical psychologist one of these days soon; we don't want a blemish to stand in the way of that. Maybe she could cop a plea for going a step too far in the interests of direct psychological research—or losing herself in her thesis—but I know, and she knows I know, that in fact she just got a little lost in Belinda. I doubt she'll get lost again.

Kid likes my house, you know.

That place could become a home, someday.

Well... enough already. I have not slept for two days. I just now hung out the Do Not Disturb, and I hope to sleep 'til luau time.

This Copp is not for hire 'til further notice.

Aloha. Peace. Go for it.